Deathbed Confession:

My Son Was A Stolen Baby!

By Danielle Parks

This book is dedicated to the people who suffer in the day-to-day as a result of being victimized; please know you are not alone. This story was inspired by actual events which drove me to find healing. Although fiction, it tells my version of how to survive through hope.

Own what happened, never be ashamed of it, speak about it, and heal from facing it. The writing of this book was cathartic and spawned the hope that anyone suffering will find a table to feast at, a place where they belong.

Danielle Parks

Chapter 1 --------------------------------------7

Chapter 2 --------------------------------------19

Chapter 3 --------------------------------------25

Chapter 4 --------------------------------------59

Chapter 5 --------------------------------------75

Chapter 6 --------------------------------------99

Chapter 7 --------------------------------------121

Chapter 8 --------------------------------------131

Chapter 9 --------------------------------------161

Chapter 10 --------------------------------------191

Chapter 11 --------------------------------------215

Chapter 12 --------------------------------------227

Chapter 13 --------------------------------------233

Chapter 14 --------------------------------------239

Chapter 15 --------------------------------------247

Chapter 16 --------------------------------------259

Chapter 17 --------------------------------------273

Chapter 18 --------------------------------------283

Chapter 19 --------------------------------------291

Chapter 20 --------------------------------------299

Chapter 21 --------------------------------------307

The End --------------------------------------311

Chapter 1

It was October 27, 1986, a day cold and dreary, heavy clouds hanging low to the ground. The moisture surrounding us took up residence on the edge of every surface, an appropriate day to attend a funeral. It was unusual weather for this time of year in Texas; the environment was somewhat dank and imposing. It was as if mother nature herself was melancholy, acknowledging the loss of a sad life that appeared to have offered no value. When inhaled, the air was stringent on the lungs, causing a mild stinging upon intake and producing a whirl of smoke when returned to the atmosphere. The troposphere around us might at any moment alter its state from a dense wet mist into snow, providing a white blanket of implied lace. An ode to the woman being laid to rest. As we lingered around the newly-opened hole in the earth, artificial turf covering the recently unearthed ground offered the pretense the wet soil had not been violated. It was here, next to the mound of fresh dirt, my family gathered to bury Mary Bennett, the woman known to me as Grandmother.

The weather offered a Toulouse Lautrec painting influence to the event; a sad picture in hues of warm grey and teals with hints of sandy-colored brush strokes mixed on a textured canvas. A sad representation of a forlorn woman living a life filled with distress. A portrait representing who grandmother was, a woman cold and imposing, yet somehow serving a purpose.

Beyond her deep devotion to my father, I could not provide a single clue what function this woman could have served. Her narrow focus of love for him guided his every move without his knowledge; the intense focus was made pointedly clear at this event. Gazing around at the guests attending this final act acknowledging her life, I noted only family in attendance. Perhaps it was due to her age, probably due to her husbands being long ago buried, her parents no longer on this planet, siblings non-existent. Any friends made, if they existed, most likely already passed on to their greater journey. Or maybe, it was a result of her always being the cold woman I grew up knowing; a woman who never managed to garner a friendship beyond superficial needs.

It is important to note thad Grandmother did not tolerate terms of endearment such as Nana or Granny; the use of these nouns was foolish to her and served no purpose. My siblings and I knew her specifically as Grand-mother; we were taught at a very early age that grand-mother was the only name acceptable to her. Her house was always pristine, never a speck of dirt found inside of doors, ne'er a crumb on a kitchen countertop or floor. Drapes perfectly hung, drawn every evening at the same time. Floors polished to a reflective sheen, rugs perfectly squared at each corner. I vividly recall the bright yellow striped linen drapes in her living room, precisely opened and closed each day, every fold in the exact same place as the day before. In my early teenage years, while being influenced by science fiction novels, I imagined her being guided by a demonic overlord. Commanding her to complete these tasks every day or else the world would suffer. As I grew into my college years, I came to under-stand this behavior and its root cause. Honestly, I never knew the tragedies thrust upon her in her youth, their impact on her life, or her actions. The atrocities cast upon her as a young girl, naive and insecure, would not be revealed until much later in my life.

The service was short in length, performed by an unruly minister whom no one in the family knew. His manner was gruff and uncaring; he mumbled as he read from the book in front of him. From a significant distance away, I could smell the cheap foul whiskey he consumed from his flask prior to the service starting. His cherub cheeks were red and scaly, I suspect from the alcohol and not the cold enveloping us. He was most likely a chaplain at the funeral home where Grandmother resided until the day of internment. For reasons I didn't understand, it was decided that only a graveside service was appropriate. The one passion my grandmother had was her love of music and dancing; I thought it odd no melodies were presented at this somber event. The final act for this woman leaving was unfitting; the celebration of life was void of music for the journey to her next adventure.

My mother maintained a proper distance from the casket. She positioned herself near the edge of the ugly, forest green canvas tent, avoiding the metal chairs with matching cushions reserved for immediate family. I stood beside her, where we managed to stay just inside the tent, just far enough under the cover to prevent the rain landing on the canopy from dripping on us. The rain made its way to the ground, where it, just as Grandmother, would be consumed by Earth.

Our distance from the graveside was one of propriety; my mother and grandmother were not fond of each other. Each of them consistently tossed blame back and forth like a table tennis volley. Each blaming the other for the way my father behaved. Dad's life had been a series of mishaps and poor choices, never ill-intentioned, but most often resulting in some form of chaos. My parents divorced several years earlier, and, to my knowledge, Mother and Grandmother had not spoken since my parents parted ways. My parents rarely spoke unless it was to argue over something myself or one of my siblings had done. It was unfortunate these two people could not agree to a life of friendship and move past the pain incurred by each of them. I was somewhat surprised, yet delighted, to see my mother at the funeral. Mom was an extremely proud southern woman of French descent who could hold a grudge longer than it takes to grow a redwood tree. I never knew if she was there to pay her last respects or was merely eliminating the opportunity for people to talk about her for not showing up. In his smug, gravelly voice, the pastor spoke of forgiveness and the usual "in a better place now" liturgy. I suppose there is a ministry class where men of the cloth are taught to make the family feel better with these statements. However well-intentioned, I find them to be hugely inadequate in someone's time of loss and grief. If this man knew the discord existing in this family, he might have recused himself from participating or perhaps had another sip from his small metal container. In hindsight, if I had known what was coming, I would have probably taken myself out of the picture as well as partaken in a drink.

Grandmother was placed in a beautiful cream-colored metal coffin and laid next to her first husband, their graves in the small west Texas town they lived in when he passed. She left this town after he died in a mysterious accident at his place of employment. Grandmother never discussed the proceedings leading up to his death; Dad was in the hospital at the time of his father's death, leaving him with little memory surrounding the event. Grandmother remarried a few years later; her second husband was kind and rather dull; this suited my grandmother very well. I recall her saying she was content to be in a home where she would never have to move again; I didn't understand the implication at the time.

Next to the graveside, just beyond the mound of dirt with its faux grass cover, a small marker bearing the name Baby Johnson caught my eye, a somewhat faded print on a simple placard in place of a headstone that had never been set. No dates or family member names; it was as if someone had forgotten the child that lay there. I had never heard tell of a baby in the family dying and wasn't quite sure who the marker represented. I intended to ask my mother later if she knew anything about the grave. To my knowledge, Dad was an only child.

As the casket slowly descended into the ground, my father stood stoically beside the grave of his beloved mother. In sequential order of birth, each of my older siblings placed a yellow rose on the casket as it was lowered. Being the youngest of the group, I participated last. Each of us kissed Dad goodbye, quietly walking away from the graveside as we knew he wanted to remain by himself. Dad was, always had been, a very private man who didn't talk about feelings. He laughed, told great jokes, and had many great friends but was as intensely personal with his life, just as his mother had been. I suspect this is why none of his friends attended the service.

There were no limousines or town cars to return everyone to their home and no family gathering with ridiculous amounts of food piled on a table. No opportunity to sup while commiserating about the life recently ended. The attendees merely postponed their commitments long enough to observe the last rights of a family member before returning to their daily responsibilities. It wasn't that we didn't love the woman — we just didn't connect with her. This made the loss lack any real emotion. After I kissed my dad goodbye, I walked through the heavy mist toward my mom, who had remained distant from participation. I immediately observed an exquisite set of jewelry she was wearing when I faced her head-on. My mother was not a woman of high fashion; she was always dressed appropriately for the occasion but maintained an understated style. The only lavish thing she ever wore was an out-of-fashion fur coat left to her by a great-aunt who died many years ago. In the years after her divorce, she focused on raising her family and not spending money on clothes, shoes, or especially jewelry. I snapped a mental picture of her that day, looking so elegant and refined. After passing the metal chairs, my shoes soggy, leaving my feet cold, I reached my mother. I took her hand, placing it firmly in mine, entwined our fingers, and held tight as we trudged through the oversaturated cemetery grass to her car. I intended to ask about the placard for the baby when she turned the conversation to the weather. She was gently suggesting the dialogue not hold anything substantive. This bothered me deeply; this sad day in our lives needed outward emotion to express our grief. It felt as if we had attended the burial of someone's beloved pet: an event important to them but with no emotional stake in it for the attendees.

As I opened the door of the Buick for my mom, I stopped. Blocking her entrance into the driver's seat, I pulled her tightly into a hug and thanked her for coming.

"It means a lot to me that you came today; I hope you know that."

She smiled at me and returned the hug.

I stepped back and purposefully stared at her.

"I am loving the necklace and earrings; very chic. I don't believe I have ever seen you wear them before."

There was a long pause, her stare sizing me up while she carefully chose her words.

"I haven't worn them before today. These were your grandmother's; I wore them today in her honor. Your grandmother was a miserable woman, and I didn't understand, until recently, what pain she carried most of her life. These were given to me the day she passed. Just before she died, your dad called me and asked that I spend some time with Mary. I didn't understand but felt I owed it to the two of them. I visited her a few times in the hospital during her final days."

I suppose the stunned look on my face revealed the thoughts going through my head.

"The last weeks of your grandmother's life were horrific for her and your father. The cancer had ravaged her body to the point she had been reduced to a skeleton maintaining a pulse. Her physicians diagnosed the cancer in her brain had metastasized. New tumors setting up residence in her major organs."

My mother talked of how Grandmother moved in and out of consciousness due to the meds administered to her. The disease had overtaken her body and mind.

"Her moments of lucidity were rare, but when she was with me, she was spot on."

I began to wonder if my grandmother had given the jewelry to my mother in one of her moments of morphine-induced thoughts. Then it dawned on me Dad would have been the one to retrieve the jewelry and deliver it to his mother at her beckoning, so all had been planned.

My grandmother sustained life longer than anyone anticipated, she wasn't ready to go, and no one knew the reason why. Her body functioning at a minimum level, pain radiating from most parts of her. She made the decision early on there would be no life support, yet she continued to hang on. When Mary Bennett finally passed, her only child was there by her side. My mother made sure I was aware my grandmother gently kissed my dad on the cheek, whispering to him before closing her eyes for the last time. My mother believed Grandmother finally achieved the inner peace she sought before she passed.

Mary Smith Johnson Bennett moved on from this world, knowing she had revealed a truth long hidden.

Chapter 2

I was twenty-two years old, working my first big boy job in a small company in the city where I grew up. I had recently returned home from college and was seeking my path. Adhering to a quote from Mame Dennis,

"Life is a banquet, and most poor sons of bitches are starving to death."

I always seemed to be looking for a banquet table I could feast at. I carried this mantra with me in life while I searched.

It was a beautiful spring day in Texas, early March if my memory serves me well, flowers blossoming, trees wearing their recently sprouted leaves like a new store-bought dress, the smell of fresh blooms emitting their lovely soft fragrance into the air. Something about the renewal of the earth each spring opened my mind and heart to the world around me, offering new perspectives and dreams. Hope was being renewed, the imposing winter blues melting away like the last bits of winter snow, and with it, I hoped the sadness which had been consuming me. It had been six months since my grandmother's funeral, and I didn't feel at a loss for her. Yet something was constantly nagging at me, pulling me towards a despair I couldn't explain, an inherent grief I couldn't shake loose. I often questioned what my mother meant when she spoke of my grandmother's great sadness. Was depression a family issue?

Unbeknownst to me, the question would be answered shortly with information that would free my soul from its constriction, just as my grandmother's spirit had finally been released from her rotting body.

Sitting at my desk on an average Tuesday morning, my colleagues and I were entrenched in our tasks at hand. The office was unusually sedate; the copiers humming, delivery men grunting on their way to the back storeroom, vending machines overhearing stories of two men's adventures the night before. All sounds I had grown accustomed to in the workplace. Ambient noise provided a background hum that somehow soothed me. With the buzzing calming me, I took a few deep breaths and settled into a narrow focus, reading a new proposal. When my desk phone rang, I halfheartedly answered, "This is Thadeus." The voice to respond was my mom's.

"Hello there, how are you?"

Her chirp reminded me of a baby bird in its nest.

She appeared more chipper than usual; a melodic tone accompanied her words, which made me suspect something was up. My mother usually presented a strong meridional demeanor, most often used when giving bad news out of left field. She was extremely adept at delivering information as if there were no significant relevance to the words she spoke. It resembled a dialogue slightly akin to a reporter who once asked,

"Other than that, Mrs. Kennedy, how was Dallas?"

This unusual perky style put me on guard.

We had a short, typically meaningless conversation. The kind I imagine most children have when starting a phone dialogue with a parent. After a few minutes of idle chatter, Mom realized I was focused on something other than her; she quickly wrapped up the phone call by requesting I have lunch with her that afternoon. This was completely out of character for her; plans were always made in advance with a step-by-step approach, like an outline for a thesis. I sensed there was a train moving towards me at great speed, me being focused on the light at the end of the tunnel, which very well could be the headlight on the engine. Mom always managed to be gracious should you stop by her house unannounced, but she never left home without a plan. I tenaciously accepted her offer and, forty-five minutes later, was sitting opposite her at a local bistro I frequented. The food was always comforting, and a glass of wine was readily available should I require it after hearing why she was there. The owners of the bistro were friends of mine; this alliance provided me with confidence that whatever she wanted to talk about would not turn into a scene, as social protocol was essential to her way of being.

We ordered iced tea and began a conversation I will be able to quote for the rest of my life, word for word. This lunch is etched in my mind as if it happened yesterday; the phrasing, the pauses, intonation of syllables.

This is how she began:

"You're old enough to know the truth now."

One stops and breathes deeply, seeking composure when a parent presents a statement like that. Scenarios abundantly flew through my head. My appearance and actions (unfortunate at times) were spot on to my mother's, so the question that I might be adopted was answered in milliseconds. I looked around the room, trying to spot a grounding rod, something to confirm this was reality and not a dream sequence I would soon wake from. Perhaps my father was not really my dad? Somewhat believable based on their love/hate marriage. The cemetery placard I saw next to Grandmother's grave with "Baby Johnson" etched on the paper immediately popped into my head. Did Dad have a sibling? Did I have a twin? What in the world was she leading up to? It was during this diatribe of pedantic ranting in my head I noticed she had Grandmother's jewelry on again. The same set she wore to the funeral.

After what seemed like ten minutes of scenarios populating my head, she looked me square in the eye.

"Your grandmother and grandfather were not who you think they were. Mary and Thadeus were not your dad's biological parents; your father was a stolen baby."

Chapter 3

Beatrice Farrell was born in rural Oklahoma on February 12, 1923. Her home sat at the base of the lush Arbuckle Mountains. On the northern side of the mountains lies a beautiful slow-moving stream with a rock basin, Honey Creek. The land inherited from her father's family, suitable for farming, provided the basic needs to sustain life for a family. The property, covered with dense patches of Post Oak trees creating thick woods, provided seclusion far away from nosey outsiders. A side benefit was law enforcement was also kept at bay. The creek provided the premium water necessary for the rye whiskey made and sold by her father.

The Farrell land sat just close enough to the City to make deliveries easy but far enough away that nobody noticed who came and went. The family resided in a simple farmhouse, a couple of rooms with a wood stove for heating and cooking and a tin roof that leaked through the nail holes when it rained. A bed for mom and dad, and a room for all their offspring. The house and barn were constructed from timber surrendered by the land, rickety at best but serving its purpose. The wood floors splintered and cracked, contained gaps between the planks; this allowed cool fresh air from the earth below to penetrate the house. The feature was useful in summer but somewhat painful in winter. The windows were functional for keeping most pests outside, should they be closed. The outbuildings, shacks to be more accurate, existing on the property were located in the woods nearby the creek. Poorly constructed but built strong enough for their intended use, the shacks kept the equipment dry and, more importantly, hidden from prying eyes. The requirements were simple, three walls with a roof to prevent rain from extinguishing the fire when heating a kettle. A large clearing near the center of the parcel was a result of trees cut down and utilized to build the houses and the barns. This clearing created a suitable area for farming; the fertile land held the rich nutrients necessary to grow a sustainable garden. Food planted every spring included squash, tomatoes, okra, watermelon, and cantaloupe. Everything required to feed this simple family was grown within feet of their front porch. Chickens roamed freely, laying fresh eggs every day; the hens, which eventually slowed down on their egg production, became dinner. When it could be afforded, a hog or cow was purchased and raised for slaughter.

Two horses existed among the farm animals, each of them well-maintained. The pair were chosen based on the strength necessary to pull a plow, but equally important was their training for being ridden, if deemed necessary. Beautiful creatures in far better shape than most farm horses. They were often saddled for a ride, mostly to ensure Edgar and the animal were in sync should a quick getaway be required. It was a concern that the Model TT might prove useless in a hurried exit; the stallions were backup to cover mountainous terrain the modern new automobile was not yet capable of.

Should a visitor show up, the shacks sat far enough away from the house to be out of sight. This also minimized the family's exposure to the business at hand. Edgar made it clear to the family only he and his eldest boys were allowed at the shacks. It was imperative the existence of the buildings never be discovered by outsiders.

The Farrell clan began with the oldest boy, Johnny. He was conceived out of wedlock, by force, when Beulah was fifteen. After a shotgun wedding, a rough marriage began. It would be three years later when Leroy arrived into the clan; Aaron was born the following year. Eleven years passed before Beulah would conceive again.

It was unknown why she was not able to conceive during this time. If her body had the ability to thwart evil, then most certainly, it was her internal parts denying her husband's seed from fertilizing her eggs. Beulah despised Edgar and his nasty temper. His drunken rampages consisted of screaming at everyone for reasons no one could discern. His moods were erratic and temper vile; his disposition often shifted by a misinterpreted smirk on the face of one of the children. A simple giggle would lead to hours of beatings, moving from one child to the next, regardless of age, only to end when he tired or sobered up. Beulah, on occasion, would defend the children, only to be beaten and sexually abused as well.

The day Beulah realized she was with child after 11 years of being barren, she wept. This discovery produced tears large and plentiful enough to replace the water in Honey Creek if it had gone dry. She prayed daily, asking to remain barren as a baby was not needed in this house. She was often forced to submit to her husband's needs at his will; after he would finish himself off with the use of her body, she implored the heavens to let her remain barren. It was not to be a part of the greater plan as life found a way. This time, it was to be a girl who would carry the name Beatrice. This child would be special beyond any of the family's imagination.

The sadness of being pregnant and her hormones out of control gave Beulah cause to speak to the baby every day. Telling the fetus to be strong and find a life better than what she could offer. This pregnancy was hard on Beulah; the brutal work on the farm, in addition to the heartache she carried, made the months drag by. Her worst fears were confirmed the day Beatrice arrived; Beulah was keenly aware of how men viewed women as property and nothing more. With a young girl in the home, she hoped the kindness she attempted to instill in her boys would be enough to protect Beatrice. Her husband knew nothing of patience or empathy. She hoped love and compassion would become a part of her boys' mindset.

Beatrice was a happy baby requiring little attention, growing quickly in her first few months. She was constantly observing her surroundings, appearing to take in the activities around her. It was on her three-month birthday, the first of many tragedies struck the Farrell farm.

The spring weather had been unusually wet, with seemingly endless rounds of heavy rain daily. The land soaked beyond saturation, the fields filled with standing water, dirt clinging to every surface while remaining slick to the touch. The red Oklahoma mud clung to each thing as if there was thatch within. Bonding to the horses' hooves, their steps labored and off-point.

With spring quickly passing and summer almost upon them, there was a significant danger the Farrells might miss the growing season for their large garden. Should they miss planting on time, the frost in the fall would ruin the produce, possibly leaving them without enough nourishment to survive the winter months. Late in May, the rains finally ceased long enough to attempt turning the land for planting. Johnny, at the hard hand of his father, prepared the horses and plows to turn the soil. The freshly cast shoes were nailed to the hooves of each horse in futility. Each step in the muck added another layer of slippery dirt on the metallic shoe. Every few feet, Johnny would stop the plow to clean the animals' hooves. A seemingly useless attempt to gain traction.

Like most days on the farm, the work was long and hard; the wet soil increased the intensity of the chore being performed. The sun sat high overhead that afternoon, beating down on the farm and all the inhabitants. The humidity was miserably high due to all the spring rains. Mosquitos buzzed around anything living, drinking blood like a fat man eating free food. Welts appeared on

Johnny's bare arms as he pressed forward with the plowing, the pests repeatedly gnawing on any bare flesh available. His skin, red and swollen itched endlessly; his overalls were drenched from his sweat, mixing with the heavy moisture in the air. Johnny pushed onward, never once complaining while he and the horses worked the field tirelessly.

Two rows remained before he could stop for rest. Johnny knew full well his dad would insist on planting the next morning; should he not complete the plowing before bed would mean a fate worse than death. He made the next to the last turn, finally nearing the last row in the field, when catastrophe struck. With a loud pop, a plow strap broke. Startling the mare as the leather strap snapped against her hindquarters, she reared up in an attempt to pull loose from the plow's harness. Johnny was certain if he lost the horse, his dad would see this as his fault and beat him senseless. In hopes of regaining control and calming the mare, Johnny let the plow fall into the mud, running to her. Johnny sprinted towards the mare; his footing gave way to the muck, forcing him to the ground on his backside, slipping, sliding forward with no means of stopping. The mare struggling to free herself, slipped in the mud just as he had. The harness released, causing the mare to rear up in fright a second time, her front legs flailing as she plummeted downward with a solid thud, her leg breaking. Unsustained by her broken leg, she fell quickly, landing on Johnny. His screams were out of both pain and fear; he had met a fate worse than death.

The horse lay on him, continuing to struggle, attempting to upright herself. Unaware Johnny was beneath her, she continually shifted in the dirt, inflicting more and more damage to his young body. Beulah heard the howl of pain from outside and ran from indoors. Dropping her rolling pin to leave a trail of flour on the floor behind her. Screaming out with a pain that only a mother could know, seeing her child suffering with no hope for survival. Hearing the commotion from his workhouse, Edgar casually walked across the rain-soaked land. Assessing the situation, he began cursing at everyone for the inconvenience of his work being interrupted. Showing little concern for Johnny, he ranted wildly over the loss of the horse. He screamed for Leroy to retrieve his gun; when Leroy returned with the firearm as requested, his father shot the horse in the head and turned to walk away.

Beulah, alongside her two other boys, stared out to the field, watching the horse die while realizing nothing could be done for Johnny. They would wait for death to come again. The euthanasia for the horse was quick, the suffering for the animal over while Johnny lay under the lifeless mass, crying out for help, numbness consuming his body. As the horse went limp, Beulah ran to Johnny as quickly as she could. Crawling into the wet soil with her son, she lifted his head gently onto her lap. Beulah knew death was imminent, and comfort was the only thing she could provide. Her eyes followed Edgar as he walked away, her hate for him so great she screamed out towards her husband, expressing her wish that it was him under the horse. Holding Johnny's head gently on her lap, she caressed his cheeks; they would remain in the dirt together. The cold, damp soil numbed her body in solidarity with her dying son. Seeking to provide some level of solace, Beulah began gently cooing to her child in hopes of calming his last minutes. Looking at the sadness in their mother's eyes, Aaron and Leroy were drawn to their older brother. Acknowledging the end was inevitable for their older sibling, each boy took hold of Johnny's one free hand; united in touch one final moment, the brothers shed common tears for the last time.

Edgar returned from the barn with his stud. Considering this scene to be madness, he grabbed Leroy up and away from this futile display of affection. He turned to reach for Aaron, who dodged his first attempted grasp. Aaron's refusal to leave his brother's side fueled the anger in his father. Edgar lurched towards the boy when Leroy intercepted him to spare his brother the impending wrath. Beulah fearing for Aaron's safety, called for him to go into the house and tend to Beatrice; she could be heard crying from inside. Hearing the cries of the baby girl, Edgar relented in his quest to punish Aaron. Tossing Leroy to the ground, Edgar walked away while reminding his son to haul the dead away.

"Use the stud to pull the carcasses into the woods!"

The cry heard from within the house was not one of need; it was a call of sadness. At her young age, Beatrice could not have known what happened, yet she sensed the great sadness consuming parts of the Farrell family that day. Aaron retreated as his mother had commanded; ignoring his father's orders, he walked to the wooden edifice, sprinting up the steps he entered the house. Aaron gently picked Beatrice up from where she lay and rocked her, holding her tight until she was finally calm. At this moment, a bond was created between the two of them, a bond that would last throughout their lives, a relationship that would prove a saving grace for each of them.

Death, finally hearing the begging from Johnny to be released from the pain, came and took his soul. His spirit released, quiet returned to the land. As directed by his father, Leroy used the stud to pull the carcass off Johnny, leaving his twisted corpse in the mud beside his mother. Beulah remained there with her son's lifeless body losing all track of time and space. Gently rocking his head back and forth as she had done when he was a baby. As the sun began to lower into the western sky, Beatrice began to settle. The comfort she found in her brother's arms lulled her into a deep sleep. Laying her down softly, he kissed her forehead before returning to his mother in the field. Aaron gently kneeled beside his deceased sibling and lifted his brother's limp body into his arms. The lifeless body in his arms was akin to a rag doll, arms and legs dangling, swaying without purpose in rhythm with his brother's gait as they walked away from the horrible site. With tears streaming down his face, Aaron followed his mother, past the front of their home, deep into the woods. Beulah walked in silence until she found a beautiful clearing to bury her son; he would spend eternity surrounded by trees. She hoped the earth would consume his body, feeding the trees and keeping a small part of him alive forever. Ashes to ashes, dust to dust, this was her prayer. One simple stone would mark the ground where Johnny's body had been returned to the earth.

The death of Johnny had a profound impact on the Farrell family. Leroy grew to be mean and spiteful, spending his days in the sheds working with his dad. Increasing in disdain for life, Leroy was becoming the exact replica of his father. Aaron, on the other hand, developed with kindness and love, no matter the situation. Edgar became more and more distant, further removed physically and emotionally from his family. His only focus was running the family business.

In 1927, prohibition was in full swing. The constitutional ban on the alcohol trade provided a need for underground liquor production. Alcohol consumption was viewed as a sin by pietists; this train of thought was of no concern to the Farrell family. Edgar was not a man of faith and felt it was his duty to supply those in need with what they wanted. As backwood stills provided spirits for the wet activist, Edgar was willing to participate in the coalition, ignoring the government ban. Beatrice's brothers and father did nothing but focus on alcohol production, deliveries, and sleep. The demand for grain alcohol continued to grow; the family business thrived in the backwoods of Oklahoma. Nobody bothered them as long as a full bottle of whiskey, alongside a stack of cash, was delivered to the Sheriff's office upon request.

At four and a half years old, Beatrice was the epitome of a good girl. She stayed by her mother's side, working the chores in tandem. She was fully capable of planting and picking the vegetables from their garden, washing clothes at the creek, lighting the fire for cooking, any and everything her mother did. Beatrice mimicked every activity to perfection.

It had been four years since the loss of Johnny, yet Beulah grieved him every day. It was a rare event when Edgar would touch his wife or made any carnal request of her, which she was thankful for. Beulah had hopes of not producing any more children and once said,

"I am grateful the bull visits other pastures."

She was content with the fact that he didn't want to be with her and thrilled he chose to fulfill his needs elsewhere. On occasion, he would show up unruly and drunk, cursing how he hadn't had any fulfillment that day. When this happened, Beulah resigned herself to let him crawl on top of her, thereby avoiding a beating if she denied him. It had been five months since the last incident. Much to her displeasure, Beulah was once again with child.

With her mother pregnant, even at her young age, Beatrice was now managing most of the household activities. Along with all the other skills she had learned from her mother, she was also capable of wringing a chicken's neck before cleaning and preparing the bird for dinner.

Edgar continued his separate life working and sleeping in the sheds. With production requiring the attention of her brothers, the household chores fell to the young Beatrice. Beulah had become very weak with this pregnancy and offered little physical assistance in the house. It would not have mattered if Edgar had been in the house; he wouldn't have, or allowed his sons to, help with "women's work." He had taken on a young mulatto girl who kept him company in the sheds. Utilizing her body as a pleasure tool, he also taught Leroy the carnal pleasures provided by the young girl. Beatrice was always relieved when her brothers chose to sleep elsewhere instead of in the bed they shared. Strange things happened to their bodies while they slept; she didn't like it.

Great sorrow had begun to grow in her mother's eyes, most notably when her father was around. Her mother was generally despondent most of the time, but something shifted when Edgar came into the house. It was as if someone were removing the light from her mother, turning her dark and sullen, filled with anger. This panicked Beatrice; she didn't like the sense chaos was about to form around her. Whenever she realized her father was coming near, she would run to her mom and crawl into her lap. This became a lifesaver for Edgar, as his wife secretly awaited the moment she would end his life. With his complete focus on making money, he did not concern himself with Beulah's unhappiness. He avoided her pregnancy with the use of his servant girl and whoever else he could find. Edgar was utterly unaware a sickness was consuming his wife; even if he had known, it was doubtful there would have been any concern.

During the last trimester of her pregnancy, the next tragedy struck the Farrell family. While making product deliveries to the speakeasies, Aaron was killed.

It was an average run with no warning signs of what was about to happen. The Feds had systematically been raiding joints all over Southern Oklahoma, Texas, and Arkansas; it was during one of these raids information about the Farrell family business was discovered. With a sizable amount of cash and a promise of a new life elsewhere, the government convinced a local juke joint owner, a man named Peters, to lure Aaron into a trap. It was not outside the Fed's practice to pay men off if they would disclose the whereabouts of suppliers providing sinful drink. They utilized any method they could to get to the root of the cause. If the righteous broke the law, it appeared acceptable as long as the heathens were being brought to justice. During the Prohibition era, the scale of justice seemed to be heavily tilted towards the self-appointed righteous.

Aaron was approaching his sixteenth birthday; he worked very hard and was known as the best driver around this part of Oklahoma. He had the keen sense to make quick decisions and execute them in an instant should anything go wrong. He was tall and handsome and knew how to use his looks to get him out of any situation. Aaron was six feet two inches tall with a muscled chest and arms; 223 pounds of pure beef. An ass that could crack walnuts and a set of blue eyes that could disarm even the meanest of people. His wavy black hair fell softly across his chiseled cheekbones, giving a boyish charm to the observer. He learned early on that he had a gift for satisfying people and developed its use to his advantage. He was unusually developed for his age and quickly discovered that boys and girls enjoyed his offerings. He carried no preconceived notions on what sex should be; he enjoyed the attention of all who gave it to him, along with the satisfaction of coin that was provided for his attention.

Thursday evening arrived, as per usual deliveries prior to the weekend; several deliveries were to be made. Leroy loaded the truck while Aaron dressed in his best attire for the evening rounds. Leroy despised his brother's good looks and big personality. He loathed the manual labor forced on him while his brother was in the spotlight, sent out to enjoy the world. Since Johnny's death, Edgar put all the physical requirements on Leroy, leaving the fun to be had by his handsome brother. The only pleasurable thing provided for Leroy was the sharing of his dad's whore. He hated that as well, not the sex, but the fact he was getting sloppy seconds from his awful father.

Before Aaron left home that fateful evening, he did something most unusual; he stopped by his mom's bed to kiss her goodbye. He must have sensed something was amiss, creating a feeling that he should speak his affections to her. Beulah loved this boy; she knew of his proclivities and loved him nonetheless. Aaron was a happy man, and she wanted him to move beyond this chaos they lived in. On his way out the front door, he grabbed Beatrice up into his arms and pulled her snuggly against him.

He whispered into her ear.

"I love you until the end of time, and I will take us away from this place soon."

Beatrice responded as any little girl who adored her brother would have, by wrapping her arms around his neck. She held him so tight he almost lost his breath. Beatrice had a great love for her brother; he was the only man she cared to be near. As he sat her back on the wooden floorboards of the farmhouse, he heard her say,

"I love you, Bubba."

Aaron had secretly been planning to take his mom and sister away from Honey Creek. Hiding the money he made being a gigolo, he would soon have saved enough for them to flee. His goal was to leave by the end of the year. Not trusting his family, he buried his money in a small tin box next to the marker where Johnny had been laid. He knew neither his dad nor his brother would ever go there, leaving the only risk of it being found was by his Mom or Beatrice.

Aaron left that night whistling a happy tune, following his usual routine, making drop-offs, and sometimes staying on to provide ancillary services. He successfully delivered the booze to all the regular customers without issue so far and had one last stop on the schedule; old man Peters' place.

Aaron knocked on the back door as usual, but tonight he was greeted by a man he didn't know; Mr. Peters wasn't there. Aaron thought this odd as the crotchety old Peters was always at his establishment; he didn't trust anyone else to control his business. Aaron knew full well the old man didn't like him; he often called Aaron queer to his face. Aaron didn't really care what Peters thought of him as long as he paid the bill when the jugs of booze were dropped. The bartender at Peters' place that night was odd; Aaron had never seen the guy who opened the door before that night; something was off about this man being in Peters' place. The good-looking man observed everything about the delivery man; Aaron perceived this as a flirtation. Using his charms on the new man, he smiled broadly as he flexed his muscles while lifting the crate of hooch. Coyly, he asked this stranger where the old man was. There was no response from the man standing in the doorway, only a grin. Leaving the crate on the floor, Aaron smiled at the young man and asked what else he good do to take care of him. The bartender shook his head, implying nothing; he handed the envelope full of cash to the delivery man. Aaron retreated through the door towards the delivery truck; stopping at the door, he paused and took one more look at the handsome stranger. He left the alleyway and felt a gnawing in his chest; something was off. Becoming somewhat suspicious of the evening's activities, he drove away from Peters' place, taking a different route than he usually did. He had one last stop before heading back to Honey Creek.

The Feds' plan was devised in such a manner as not to catch Aaron at the delivery but to follow him to each of his customers. The goal was to obtain complete discovery of all the speakeasies in town, eventually leading them back to the stills. What Peters was not aware of, or failed to tell the federal agents, was his shop was the last on the route.

Aaron made his final stop for the evening at a little apartment on the edge of town; this was his favorite place to be. He made it a point to regularly take time to visit his only true love before going home whenever he delivered the whiskey.

The agent following him from Peters' place knew of Aaron's sideline business as a gigolo. As he knew Aaron didn't have any more product in the truck to unload, he became compelled to let Aaron enjoy himself. He made the assertion this would be the last time Aaron would enjoy the companionship of a woman for a long time. Sitting in his car, he lit a cigar and watched Aaron enter the small apartment building.

Opening the door to his lover's apartment, a smile landed on his lips. He was welcomed by nudity on full display on the bed; the visual stimulation of seeing his lover waiting for him aroused him both physically and emotionally. Removing his clothes as he crossed the room, he joined his love in the bed.

Time passed quickly as Aaron focused on every moan produced; each audible groan of pleasure was skillfully addressed with precision. He was a master of maintaining a heightened level of lust and intimacy. The hour-long lovemaking event culminated with each lover moaning out loud as they climaxed within seconds of each other, their hot, sweaty bodies falling into a heap of flesh. Pulling his lover tightly against him, Aaron exhaled deeply into his lover's ear, sliding his tongue gently across the earlobe and ending with a kiss on the neck. With this, he relaxed. Keeping his lover as close and tight as possible, he began nuzzling the nape of his partner's neck when he realized the two were being observed from across the room. He looked up to the doorway leading to the other room, holding onto his companion lovingly; he relaxed, realizing it was his lover's wife smiling at them.

Entering the room, she crossed the floor seductively before crawling into the bed next to Aaron. She placed her bare breast against his back, filling in each curve with flesh, his round taught ass touched by her dark pubic mound, his thighs being spread by her legs sliding between them. Kissing him deeply as she reached across him, placing her hands gently on her husband's chest, the thrice of them in perfect harmony.

Aaron had begun his affair with the young couple about a year prior. It started with her, and when her husband began participating, Aaron found himself in the awkward position of falling in love with the Carter County Deputy Sheriff.

The young lawman savored the moment as he was aware this would be their last encounter with Aaron. Noticing the dawn was beginning to break, Aaron lifted himself from between the couple. Moving to the edge of the bed, he began mentally preparing himself to go back to the chaos of home.

The Sheriff's deputy gently reached out, taking Aaron's hand in his, their fingers entwined as he pulled Aaron back into the bed where the couple resided. Settling back into this cocoon of bodies, Aaron expressed his desire to stay and not return home. It was at this moment the deputy revealed the information he had overheard the day before.

The Federal officers had outlined their plans to the Sheriff the previous afternoon, unaware the young officer was sitting within earshot. Normally outside the government operating procedures, an unusual courtesy was offered up to the Sheriff. He was married to the sister of a prominent member of Congress; it had been suggested the agents provide the Sheriff enough time to clean up any messes he might be involved in before they moved in on the Farrells.

The young couple held Aaron closely as the deputy formed his words.

"There is nothing but sadness and great chaos for you and your family if you go back."

The deputy's wife placed her head against her husband's back, wrapping her arm and leg around the two men, hugging them both tightly. She clenched her hand on top of her husband's, placing pressure on Aaron's waist, pulling him closer. Speaking ever so softly, she begged Aaron to heed the warning and disappear.

Held in their embrace, Aaron reached behind him to gently stroke his two lovers, listening thoughtfully to their plea. After a few minutes of quiet, he pulled himself away, falling to the floor beside the bed; he broke their union. Observing them with a passion unknown by most, Aaron leaped back into the bed, wrapping his arms around them one last time.

Managing the emotions between lust and sadness, he stood and began to dress; additional information was presented to him while he prepared to leave. With all his clothes returned to his body, he passionately kissed his lovers goodbye, requesting a favor from them; a promise to watch over Beatrice and his mother. When the deputy acknowledged and committed to the request, Aaron exited the apartment. He walked out into the waning moonlight, quietly, slowly, deliberately making his way to the delivery truck. Crossing the street, Aaron turned to see the couple watching him from their window; stares from the handsome bartender at Peters' place accompanied their gaze from inside the black car parked across from his truck. He immediately knew the information presented to him to be true. He did not wave a final goodbye as he reached the truck; he simply took his place in the driver's seat, started the vehicle, and drove away. The handsome bartender followed him as planned. Aaron was committed to protecting the ones he loved, no matter what.

Aaron would not return home that night; kissing his mother goodbye the previous evening would be the last time they ever touched.

Beulah's sadness consumed her when Aaron didn't return. One day, two days, a week passed with no word from him. She assumed him to be dead, though it was never confirmed. The sadness took hold of her weak body, causing her to remain in bed through the rest of her pregnancy.

On a chilly morning in September, the twins arrived at the Farrell farm. The midwife had been summoned but arrived too late to assist with the birthing; the girls were born still. The pneumonia Beulah suffered from, along with her overwhelming despair for her lost son, was too much for her body. The energy wasted on her hatred towards her husband, along with the illness, returned death to the small farm. Three lives were now gone.

Beatrice named the girls Eula and Zula, rhyming their names with her mother's. With Beatrice's assistance, the midwife wrapped the babies in blankets, placing them in Beulah's cold, lifeless arms. The midwife treated the dead with all the kindness and gentility deserved, gently managing each fold of the blanket so as not to disturb the sleeping trio. After saying a prayer over the recently deceased, she disappeared into the woods to give Edgar the news. He meagerly responded,

"Okay."

He didn't return to the shack with the midwife or make any effort to console Beatrice. No heed to the young girl's despair or to his dead wife was ever made. It would be three days before someone would enter the shack and tend to the deceased residing inside the house. Beatrice remained vigilant at their side, praying for help to a god she didn't know.

It was early morning; when few in the world were awake, the servant girl snuck her brothers into the house to gather the bodies for burial. Beatrice recognized the dark-skinned girl from her father's sheds but had no clue about her purpose on the land, only that she worked in the sheds during the day and disappeared at night. Her spirit brightened when the young girl explained why they had come when Edgar was asleep. Beatrice led them through the woods to where her oldest brother was buried and asked they place the trio next to him. At her young age, she found a great appreciation for the kindness that existed in people who were treated so poorly.

She witnessed the cruelty her father imposed on the beautiful girl, how he mistreated her, yet she exuded kindness and caring for someone she didn't particularly know. Providing compassion towards a family whose father was abusing their sister spoke volumes to the young Beatrice. It taught her compassion for loving one's neighbor, no matter how heinous an offense they may have committed.

After the last full shovel of dirt had been tossed on her mother and siblings' remains, the girl's oldest brother looked to Beatrice,

"We be leaving this awful place and taking our sister away from that man tonight — you can come with us and find a new start if you want."

She kissed the boy on the cheek and spoke a gracious No, Thank You. The dark-skinned threesome walked away in the opposite direction from the shack, through the woods, past the creek, on their way to search for a better life. Beatrice sat between the graves, mindless of the time she spent letting life pass by. She sat in the morning cool, shivering, wishing the sun would rise and provide her warmth. She remained by the graves throughout the day and into the night, at a loss for what she should do. Her sadness, so vast, not even hunger, compelled her to return home. The sun long gone, Beatrice began her return to the shack.

When she neared the opening of the woods, she noticed strange men in dark suits walking around, knocking things over and cursing. She sat down quietly at the edge of the trees taking cover in the underbrush, attempting to stay hidden until they found what they were looking for and moved on. Searching under the house, looking in the barn, and opening every barrel they could find, nothing seemed to appease them. As she sat hidden in the undercover of the woods, shaking in fear, lying against the dew-covered ground, she began to question why all this sadness was laid upon her.

Deep in thought and unaware of her surroundings, she jumped when a hand touched her shoulder while another covered her mouth, muffling the yelp she emitted.

"Are they gone?"

It was Leroy.

Out of fear of her brother and partially in retaliation for scaring her, she attempted to gain freedom by biting his hand; such force exuded from her jaw that he cursed her out loud.

"You fucking bitch!"

Stepping back, he grabbed his hand to assess the damage she had done. Seeing the blood drip from the open wound, he lurched towards her in an attempt to strike her. As his hand swung backward, lights suddenly flooded the forest. Shining from every direction, spotlights illuminated where they stood at the edge of the woods. Within seconds men in suits with guns were running toward them. Leroy quietly raised his hands into the air. The men swept in like gnats on a warm summer's eve, screaming and cursing at him. Words Beatrice had never heard. One of the men grabbed her. Shaking her hard, he questioned,

"Hey! Who are you? Where did you come from?"

Instinctively she pointed back to the woods where the graves were. She didn't want to be associated with whatever it was these men wanted.

Leroy commanded,

"She's the little shit from the neighboring farm, always snooping around here."

The man dropped Beatrice to the ground. He yelled at her to leave and to never speak of what she had seen. With that, she pushed all her might to her legs and ran towards the graves, past them, until she knew she was out of sight. She circled back to a large tree and sat down, attempting to stay hidden while managing a view of the headlights on their cars. After a long time sitting in the cold evening air, the warm light from their cars dissipated. Beatrice returned to the graves, where she snuggled into a ball on the ground between them in the hope of finding warmth and rest. Sleep evaded her; she was cold and afraid and wondered why Leroy had protected her. Going over and over the events of the evening in her head, she remained awake until, eventually, sleep overcame her cold little body.

When she awoke the next morning, she looked up to see the outline of a man standing over her. As her eyes cleared, her pupils adjusted to the morning sunlight. A man with a badge and gun came into focus above her. He asked her name and what she was doing there. The response was simply,

"Beatrice."

He leaned down to her, gently lifting her frigid body up, pulling her into his jacket to provide some warmth. He stood up to carry her back to the house, attempting to be very tender so as not to frighten her. As he moved away from the graves with her in tow, she began to fight him, pushing against him with the strength of ten men. She didn't know this man and feared what he might do to her. Finally able to free herself enough, she began to strike him with her fist. After the first blow struck his face, he knelt down and released her on the ground. Holding a firm grip on her tiny hands, he continued to kneel, remaining at eye level with her; he continued to smile.

"Aaron loves you very much; he made me promise to watch after you until the 'end of time.'"

Beatrice quickly calmed down, remembering those words coming from her brother's mouth. After a moment of recovery, her body relaxed enough for the deputy to release her hands. He stood up before removing his jacket and wrapping it around her; quietly, they walked back to the house hand in hand. Walking up the wooden steps, Beatrice noticed a lovely young woman cleaning up the mess of the birth and death. She bundled all the soiled linens for discarding before utilizing a pail filled with water and borax to scrub the stains on the floor. Beatrice took a seat in the rocking chair her mother had used, observing the woman as she worked.

Meanwhile, the bedding and clothes were taken outside and burned by the deputy. Slowly rocking in the chair, Beatrice was in awe of this beautiful woman working furiously to remove the red stains from the wooden floor. When satisfied with the results, the woman placed all the scrubbing utensils in the bucket. Putting the cleaning items on the back porch, the deputy's wife then turned her attention to Beatrice. Taking her by the hand, she led Beatrice down to the creek to bathe her. She washed the young girl's hair, gently combing it to remove the wooden elements acquired from sleeping in the woods. The slow-moving water was chilled, causing both of them to shiver. They moved through the ritual as quickly as possible to minimize the cold. Dressing Beatrice in a clean pair of underwear and a simple kinder dress, the woman lifted Beatrice up to rest on her hip as she wrapped both of them in a blanket. Pulling the woolen rag tight around them, they snuggled together, seeking warmth. Beatrice had never had this treatment before: once more, the kindness of a stranger presented to her. Not requested, not wanted, but a gift nonetheless. The deputy's wife walked back to the house with Beatrice in her arms, both clinging tightly to each other within the warmth of their shroud, finding comfort for each of them. When they arrived back at the farmhouse, the man with the badge was speaking to Edgar.

"It's clear what they were looking for last night. It looks like Leroy is going to pay the price. My wife and I are on our way to Sheldon County. The Sheriff told me of last night's events this morning when he got into the station.

As we were driving this way to Sheldon, I wanted to pay you a visit to get your side of the story. When we got here, we found her sitting in the cold."

Edgar was silent for a moment, quietly sizing up the deputy and the woman. They could be a decoy for the Feds trying to get more information.

"Don't know where the wife is. Must've runoff during it all."

Edgar became very jovial with the man, trying to cast a friendly hook to lure more information. This behavior was utterly foreign to Beatrice and, she thought, entirely out of her father's character. What was her father up to? Surely, he noticed the house had been cleaned and the bodies removed.

"My wife cleaned her up and gave her some clothes we collected for the children's home."

The deputy spoke, not wanting anyone to suspect his real reason for being there.

No one could know about his relationship or his promise to Aaron.

"Should we take her with us until your wife returns?"

Edgar quickly responded.

"No, she can manage the house until she comes back. If they come back."

Interested in the response, the deputy inquired further.

"They?"

"Hell—I am guessing the wife ran off with my colored whore —she has disappeared too."

Taking heed, the young lawman determined it was best to leave for now and lay out a plan to ensure Beatrice's safety and get her out of there when the time was right. He was aware of the business dealing here on Honey Creek and felt it was best to be thought ignorant to such things.

"Ok then, we will leave you to it. Come on, Ida, let's get on to the orphanage. Good day to you all."

The deputy winked at Beatrice; his signal gave her a small sense of hope that all would be fine. As the young couple drove off in the police cruiser, Beatrice's father told her to stay out of his way going forward. His statement made it quite clear her responsibilities were to make sure food was produced and served - nothing else. He would run the business by himself from that point on.

And that's how it was for the next eight and a half years.

Chapter 4

Mary's life in Oklahoma City was not what she imagined. She had all the things one could want in 1934. A home with a Frigidaire, indoor plumbing, and a husband who provided for her— sort of. She was aware she would never have children and had grown accustomed to the agonizing desire for a child that never ceased. Bearing and raising children of her own wasn't to be a part of her life; sad as it was, it was a reality she lived with. Mary was overwhelmed when six years back, Thadeus asked her to marry him. Knowing full well she was not able to provide him offspring; she had been completely upfront with him about her sterility. Mary felt if she hid this truth from Thadeus, he would find out sooner or later. She didn't want to live with that anxiety continually hanging over her head. She kept enough secrets from the world and felt confiding this single detail to him made her appear connected to him. In divulging her secret to him, she explained she was also unable to participate in sexual activities. This led to an agreement between them; he was permitted liaisons outside the marriage, provided no children were sired and romance never blossomed with anyone else. Somehow this agreement made it easier for Thadeus to enter into marriage; he had never wanted children anyway. This ensured home and hearth without little ones would never be a concern. He acknowledged to himself this was selfish; children would mean altering the life he lived and would ultimately mean danger for them due to the choices he made.

Mary never questioned his reasons; she accepted it as a sign from above when he agreed to have a life with her, no matter her past or the conditions imposed. Thadeus was, all in all, an adequate provider, and Mary was grateful for the life she was leading, for the most part. She wore the latest couture and kept weekly appointments at the beauty shop. All that a decent, upstanding lady in the City could want. She was provided a weekly allowance to spend however she saw fit. She wasn't allowed anything additional, and Thadeus often questioned himself how she could afford the dresses she wore. Her closet was full of stylish wraps and skirts paralleling the fashions of Europe. She never asked for additional money, and he never received bills from the department stores; he chose to leave well enough alone.

He managed their finances and paid all the bills; it was his way of controlling what she did and warding off questions concerning their financial status. Considering he had no real job that anyone could tell, they lived an upper-middle-class life. He felt it was best to keep Mary in the dark about certain activities; this kept her safe and minimized the risk of her saying anything that might cause an eyebrow to rise. Mary had learned in her youth, men didn't like to be questioned. She had served time in a home with a beast that controlled every moment, every movement, all the way down to their souls. At least here, she was not beaten if she did anything he might deem inappropriate.

The payment for this life was loneliness and silence. Mary was not allowed to ask where he was going at any time of the day. When he came home at three or four in the morning, no discussions were to be had. She was completely unaware of her husband's business dealings. She had never witnessed him with a temper, but something deep inside her whispered it was best she did not find out if he had one. The other requirement from Thadeus was his house be immaculate at all times, his clothes freshly pressed each day, and dinner on the table at the same time every evening. These requirements were no problem for Mary as she had a condition that forced her to seek perfection on every level. She cleaned incessantly; a speck of dirt on the floor meant the broom and mop were put to use, and the mop water changed every time it slightly darkened. A dishtowel not folded or a weed in the flowerbed would send her into a panic. She didn't understand the behavior; it was just who she was and had been since she was a teenager.

Clothes were pressed to perfection, and Thadeus always left the house looking sharp. He wore shoes shined to a mirror finish, spats entirely white without a mark, and pants the perfect length with creases as sharp as razors. His shirts were of the finest cotton found in the City, with his cuffs turned exactly at the ridge on his wrist, thoroughly starched to inhibit the formation of a wrinkle. Exquisite meals were prepared every evening just for the two of them. Leftovers were most often utilized for her during her solo lunches.

Mary was an accomplished seamstress; she stitched all her dresses and wraps. Keeping her and her husband well-tailored was just another part of her obsession. Thadeus liked that Mary could repair his garments when they were unexpectedly torn or clean them should they acquire an unknown spot of dirt or blood. She didn't like the implications the stains on his clothing suggested, but she would obsessively scrub them free from their carrier. She asserted it was easier to perform this task at home rather than make excuses to the dry cleaners or tailor. Thadeus never made the connection his wife was a talented seamstress; he was too busy with himself to realize her abilities.

Mary's body was slender and seductive, with all the curves in the right places, just like the Monaco Grand Prix. Anything she made would be sewn repeatedly until the fabric fit her body perfectly. This was indeed not vanity but her unrelenting need for perfection caused by her illness. Mary had been blessed with beautiful brown almond-shaped eyes with flecks of gold mixed among varying shades of sand and mud, all perfectly blended. If you looked deep enough, you could see a brown flowing river bed within them. Her long black eyelashes naturally curled slightly upward, and when she added a touch of mascara, it appeared she might be wearing false eyelashes. Milky skin without a blemish, ample sinewy breasts, thick, voluptuous thighs accented by a small waistline. Her feet slim with the toes of a pinwheel, perfectly shaped and pointed, ne'er a callous anywhere to be found. Her toes were always painted meticulously. Her hair was cut to precision and beautifully colored, a pale blond hue framing her soft glowing face, further enhanced with just enough lip and rouge color to augment her appearance. This never changed! Should she gain a pound, she would starve herself until that pound was gone, a compulsion that would bring her out of bed at night. She would remove all of her night garments and stand on the scale. Checking over and over until that pound was gone. When the pound disappeared, she would return to her bed and sleep only to repeat the ritual in the morning before breakfast to confirm her weight was stable. Her hair appointments were scheduled in advance and were never missed. Once, the hairdresser cut her finger so deeply that she was not able to keep the haircut and color appointment. Mary completely melted down in the shop, afraid her roots wouldn't be touched up. Without the color, people would know her hair color was enhanced and not her own. Every time her life was slightly altered, she was unable to recover without several hours of gut-wrenching tears and tantrums.

If a stranger were to observe Mary walking down Main Street, they would easily assume she was a Hollywood Starlet lost in the wrong town or perhaps here to visit family; maybe she had been born here and moved on. It was unfortunate for Mary that most of the women in the City knew who her husband was and therefore paid little to no attention to her. Thadeus had a reputation for underhanded dealings and using powers of persuasion to get his way. Thadeus was thankful for Mary's peculiar behavior, as he reasoned others would not engage her, protecting the life he worked so hard to create.

Another of Mary's oddities was her fear of automobiles; she refused to learn to drive and was a nervous mess when she rode in one. Thadeus never asked why his wife didn't want to learn to drive; he was quite happy she preferred to take the bus. This provided him certainty Mary wouldn't go anywhere beyond the hairdresser, Woolworths, or home. This routine gave Thadeus a sense of relief they would never cross paths while he was working.

Due to the reputation of her husband, people avoided Mary at all costs. Social clubs ignored her request to join or attend a meeting. Mary internalized the rejection determining it was her. Even though she was perfection to the outsiders' eyes, all she saw in the mirror was the girl from long ago, taken advantage of and altered for all eternity. Mary was firm in her belief that only two people in Oklahoma City could ever know her dirty little secret. She trusted these people with undying faith. She kept her shame close by and never spoke of it to anyone else, including her husband. The only genuinely kind, non-judgmental people she knew were Mrs. Simpson and her divine hairdresser, Eunice. These women were her trusted confidants who would never share her secret. Yet she was never sure why the ladies she attempted to engage ignored and shunned her. She was clueless; her husband was the reason she was considered a social deviant and left out of social circles.

As each day passed, her neuroses grew. The house had begun to close in on her; she couldn't clean it deep enough. Time spent at home allowed for more and more items to be found, each item requiring a cleaning. The white grout on the kitchen tile was beginning to wear through in certain spots due to her obsessive scrubbing ritual. She was starting to see the underlayment as she couldn't stop scouring the grout. This caused her more stress as she knew it would have to be repaired, and she didn't want her husband to see why she was losing what sanity she had. Finally, an option appeared to her from the paper; reading the Oklahoman Daily, she noticed an advertisement for a seamstress in a tailor shop on the far edge of town. The shop was to be opened in a popular up-and-coming area. E. K. Gaylord himself called the suburb the greatest expansion the city would ever see. Mary had confidence in herself when it came to sewing; believing she was an excellent seamstress, she decided to apply for the job. Mary assumed the suburb lay far enough away from home her husband would never see her there. With the shop being new and a fair distance away, she figured the owners wouldn't have heard of her or her eccentricities. It was a safe assumption that in a town with a population of 204,000 people, no one in the new suburb south of Grand Boulevard would know who she was. Laying out her Ben Franklin list of pros and cons for working outside the home, she concluded it was necessary for her to acquire a means of independence. Her entire life had lacked free will; it was now time she sought a path all her own. With that, she arose from the table, cleaned the kitchen from breakfast, made the bed, and prepared herself for an adventure. Thadeus had left early that day, providing her some comfort and enough confidence to follow through with her plan. She laid out her finest blue satin dress; she then coordinated shoes, belt, and handbag to match. Assessing her look in the vanity mirror, Mary decided to complete the ensemble with a broad-brimmed hat made from the leftover satin of her dress. Off to the bus stop she went. It seemed miles and miles passed while on the bus before she arrived at her destination; it was further from where she began on Thirty-Sixth Street than she had imagined. While on the bus, she observed the City, seeing it in a way she had not before (it should be noted natives of Oklahoma often referred to their capital as merely, The City). She was amazed at how the City had grown and began to question all she was missing; life was happening around her, and she was not aware. Arriving at her stop, she stood up, taking a moment to smooth out her perfectly fitted dress; she exited the bus with her head held high. Standing on the pavement, looking at her new surroundings, she realized she was stuck in her own small little world. She was determined to broaden her perspective; with that thought, she took the next steps in her journey.

According to her map, the bus route ended three blocks from her destination. She gingerly stepped on the freshly poured, unscarred sidewalk, proceeding slowly, taking in all the new buildings. So crisp and clean, fresh new paint butting up against rough red Chicago bricks. Shiny new windows, so clean they appeared transparent as if nothing separated indoors and out. As she began to walk towards the tailor shop, she caught a glimpse of herself in a furniture shop window.

Full-length vanity mirrors were on display in the shop window, shiny new silver backs perfectly reflecting the outside world. At first glance, she didn't realize it was her in the mirror. She thought it to be a mannequin wearing an outfit made for a lady. The figure looking back at her was stunning; a well-dressed woman with a perfect body was in the reflection; apparently, a woman loved and provided for. She stopped to admire the porcelain figure with great admiration. The moment quickly passed when she became aware of the stunning creature in the window was she; within milliseconds, the woman in the reflection shifted and was again a tattered, ragged, dirty girl. There was nothing she could do on the outside to fix the nasty, grotesque being she was. Slowly her eyes looked down, avoiding the reflection in front of her; there she stood for several minutes staring at the street. Standing there in a trance of despair, transfixed in this mind-numbing moment of her reality, her demon continued beating her down. Unaware of her surroundings, she heard a soft muffled voice question if she was all right. She was caught off guard by a hand touching her shoulder, startling her back to reality. She looked up, and there, in front of her, stood a woman with the kindest cherub face she had ever seen, beaming with sympathy and compassion.

"Dear sweet girl, is there something I can help you with?"

Mary stood there, silently shaking her head from side to side, answering in the negative.

"I am Mrs. Pfeifer. I think we should take you to sit down. I am not sure you are all together at the moment."

Mary pulled herself back to her current reality.

"Oh yes, ma'am, I am fine. I have come to apply for the seamstress job in the new tailor shop and felt as if I were lost for a moment."

Lottie Bell Pfeifer smiled with complete surprise while contemplating why this woman would be applying for a job.

"What's your name, dear?"

"Mary Johnson. I live in the City and am in desperate need of work. The shops in town all have their positions filled, and I thought this would be a great place to be. Surely with the growth of the city, there will be plenty of work in Moore."

Lottie Bell shifted her stance, sensing the desperation in Mary. She could see a sincere desire within her, believing this woman needed help.

"Are you married, dear?"

"Yes, Ma'am. My husband works, but with the rumblings of war overseas, we are looking to save some money just in case he is called up to serve."

"Well, come on dear, I own the shop with my husband. Let's go talk to Herbert. The shop is mine, but my husband insists on interviewing anyone who might work with us. I have managed to keep him out of trouble for the last 15 years, and yet he thinks I can't manage to hire someone who won't take advantage of me. Do you have any examples of your work to show?"

"Yes, Ma'am."

Mary replied while smoothing the wrinkles from her dress.

"Call me Lottie Bell. I am not old enough to be a 'ma'am' to you."

She giggled slightly as she spoke. Lottie Bell didn't believe in traditional realities or man-made requirements. She had been a dancer in her early days and knew way more about life and men than most of the women in Oklahoma City. Her husband had proven himself a wild man in WW1, returning to Boston after the war ended. When Herbert found her at the end of his tour, he snatched her up and took her far away from the chaos of Boston. After trying out several places in the Midwest, they chose to settle here, a new frontier, if you will. A place where they could make their own rules and not be held to the piety of the eastern seaboard. Herbert Pfeifer promised her a life of happiness and adventure, and here they were with a business of their own, calling the shots as they saw fit.

As they walked into the shop, Lottie Bell bellowed for her husband. He came from the back of the shop with a pipe half packed and asked what the hell she was yelling for. After cursing at his wife for interrupting his quiet time, he noticed Mary and quickly apologized for the language. This open honesty between them put Mary at ease; she felt oddly comfortable around these strangers. No pretense, no show, just two people living a life together in an uncomplicated manner. The love they shared was palpable.

Lottie Bell looked up at Herbert.

"If you are done being an ass, this lovely young lady has come to apply for the seamstress job."

Herbert excused himself while walking to the back of the shop; he returned a few moments later wearing a proper shirt and tie to conduct the interview. For Mary, the meeting seemed to be hours worth of questions that had nothing to do with her capabilities. Herbert was a tough man, but Mary sensed he was a man who always did the right thing, regardless of how unpopular it was. After the endless questions, Mary repaired a dress that had been torn and moved on to hem a pair of men's trousers, complete with cuffs. After a thorough inspection of the repairs, the offer was made to hire her. They agreed to a salary and hours of work. Mary would work from 9:00 a.m. to 3:30 p.m. Monday through Thursday, the hours carved out perfectly to coincide with the bus schedule. Herbert questioned why she didn't drive, Mary explained she and her husband had the one car, and her husband required it for his job.

"Besides, who has two cars?"

A true statement to support her deceit as to why more money was needed. She hoped by balancing the lies; she was believable. Working this schedule would allow her to arrive home in time to take care of the house, cook dinner, clean, and be ready for Thadeus when he came home. She had no intention of telling Thadeus about her new job. She needed to exercise some independence, confident he would not allow her to work or have her own money; this was the only way.

It was only a small, white lie, she thought.

Chapter 5

Thirteen and a half years of life had passed for Beatrice living on that farm in southern Oklahoma. Since the death of her mother, the disappearance of Aaron, and Leroy going to prison, her life has been solitary, with the exception of the minimal time spent with her dad. She was thankful every day for small favors from the heavens but mostly for the limited interaction with her father. Knowing it would cause unnecessary rage leading to a heated battle, she never asked for anything from Edgar. Christmas and birthdays were events celebrated by other people; holidays were non-existent in her house. She wasn't exactly sure when she was born; there was no birth certificate or records to review, only bits of information garnered from her father when he spoke to someone visiting the farm. She counted the years since her last birthday with her mom and believed she to be 14 years of age. A bright spot in her day-to-day was when, on occasion, the Carter County Sheriff would stop to visit. Beatrice noted a pattern to his visits; he always managed to come around when Edgar wasn't home. She assumed the Sheriff didn't want to be near her father any more than she did. The Sheriff had always been a friendly man to her; he was very handsome and had a kind heart. He never asked her for anything, just sat and talked. Beatrice vividly remembered the young deputy's wife, who cleaned her up after her momma died.

The previous Sheriff disappeared around that same time, leaving this man in control of the county where she lived. She felt she could trust him no matter what, although she always wondered how he knew Aaron and never could quite discern how he knew where she lived. In her mind, the little farm was so far removed from the road and hidden by the trees that only people who had business with Edgar knew where the farm was.

On his visits, the Sheriff would bring books and paper to Beatrice, hoping to promote a desire in her for learning. He would spend time with her sounding out the words in the new books. She once heard him argue with Edgar about her being old enough to attend school in their little town; Edgar said she was better off stupid and would not go. It wasn't until Beatrice learned to read that she began to understand what her father meant. Anything Sheriff Turner brought to her for studies was quickly hidden from her father; she felt it was best he thought her stupid. The books and ledgers traveled back with the

Sheriff to his wife for review and corrections. Beatrice was incredibly adept at writing and reading for her age. The question of a formal education had been squelched by her father, leaving Sheriff Turner and his wife to find a path to expose her to an education by whatever means necessary. They believed this to be a part of fulfilling their promise made to her brother.

In the spring of 1936, the Great Depression was taking its toll on the poor. Some men had found work under FDR's New Deal, but most were unskilled, uninterested, or unable to land a job. These men were Edgar's best customers. Beatrice heard stories from her dad's clients on how tough it was to find work and how they barely had enough food to feed their families. Their stories were no different from the life she had always known, so she couldn't understand what their complaining was about. She found it very interesting that people spoke of not having money to feed their kinfolk but somehow managed cash for gas in their cars and enough extra to buy Edgar's homemade juice. If a customer ever noticed her and commented on her presence, Edgar would quickly dismiss the conversation and shoo her away. Never once did anyone question why this young girl was seemingly all alone with him.

Beatrice began to notice changes in her body she didn't understand. Hair was growing in places she never expected follicles to exist. First her underarms, then between her legs. Her shins covered with soft down-like fur, and the new hair growth she didn't understand caused her to panic. Her chest was swelling and tender to her touch; the circles on her chest were darkening and growing sensitive, creating a significant concern in her. Her lean and lanky frame enhanced the noticeable swelling of her breast. These changes made her uncomfortable, but she did her best to hide them from her father.

Beatrice managed a small patch of land in front of their house where the garden was. The once large area plowed for farming was now significantly reduced and overgrown. If you looked carefully into the field while standing on the front porch, you could see remnants of a plow upside down in the dirt. She once asked her father why it was there; his response was simply that she should mind her own business.

Her days were spent working the land to produce vegetables, along with tending the chickens. With no help to speak of, it was a battle to keep food on the table. Between the jackrabbits eating the garden and the coyotes taking chickens away during the night, she somehow managed enough food to feed her and her father. Edgar would often exchange his gallons of brew for household necessities such as sugar, flour, and salt. Rarely did they enjoy pork or beef; their diet consisted mostly of items readily available on the farm. With no cows or hogs to contend with, the bulk of the farm was neglected. Left to be overgrown and ignored, much like her.

During one of Sheriff Turner's visits, he observed the two round mounds of flesh on Beatrice's chest; he was surprised to see she had developed so quickly since his last visit. Looking for other signs, he noticed the soft down-like hair on her legs and arms. He concluded she was around the age to start puberty. Aaron had never disclosed how old his sister was; it seemed strange that so many years had passed for all of them. Sheriff Turner's stopover was to tell Edgar that Leroy was being released from prison in four weeks; he would need to be picked up. As he delivered this news to Edgar, he quickly connected the possibilities of Beatrice's impending womanhood and a brother returning home from prison. He became sorely afraid for her.

Sheriff Turner warned Edgar,

"If no one is there to get him, he'll be sent to Oklahoma City to start a new life. Without a family member claiming him, he will be sent to live in a home and be monitored for behavioral issues."

The Sheriff hoped Edgar wouldn't care and would leave the boy to start anew outside of Carter County. As the Sheriff watched for a response, he was shocked and saddened to see Edgar light up with the news that Leroy would soon be out of prison. Beatrice wasn't sure if he was excited to have his son back home or if it was that he needed someone to help with the stills. Whatever the reason, her father appeared to be happy. She stood nearby and listened as they traded information, she patiently waited for the Sheriff to acknowledge her, but alas, he didn't speak to Beatrice on this visit. He remained very distant and official while presenting his notice. Once the message was delivered, the Sheriff turned heel, headed back to his car, and drove away.

Beatrice found this behavior very odd and deeply hurtful. She didn't understand why he didn't speak to her, drop off new books, or collect the ones she had finished. On every visit before this one, he had been kind and caring; this time, he appeared extremely agitated and irritable. Watching him drive off that day, her heart sank. She always hoped he would find a reason to take her away. Beatrice knew just enough from reading the books left by the Sheriff there were other places to see. She longed to discover life beyond this farm. As the Sheriff disappeared beyond the trees, her dad went to the sheds to continue packaging more booze for delivery. Once he was beyond her sight, Beatrice turned and walked past the garden, heading to the family graves. She replayed the conversation over and over in her head. Revisiting each word between the Sheriff and her father, she tried to connect the dots why she had been ignored.

Since her last visit to her mom's eternal bed, the land had become overgrown, covered with dirt and weeds. The path to the graves no longer existed. Having walked to the graves so many times over the years, the brush was of no concern. She remembered precisely the direction and distance from the house. As she approached the gravestones, something caught her eye, startling her. The rock on her mother's grave had been cleared and cleaned to sparkle like new, a fresh lily now lying upon it. No one else knew about the graves except her and the boys who buried the bodies for her. As she stood there staring at the rock with the beautiful flower on it, she noticed something even more frightful. The stone marking where Johnny was buried had also been cleared, and a tulip had been laid upon it. She immediately stopped in her tracks to look around. She peered deep and hard into the woods, looking at every angle, every shadow, every bush; nothing. She became so overwhelmed with emotion she was moved to tears. She dropped to the ground on her fuzzy knees and wept, not for the sorrow of the loss but from the joy that someone else in the world cared about her. After exhausting herself from crying, she gathered herself together and rose to her feet. She sensed she was being protected; it was as if someone was watching over her. She had felt this presence before but could never make sense of it. As she began walking back to the house, she heard a twig behind her snap. She quickly spun around and saw him, a man in a dark suit, dashing rapidly away. She was so bewildered she couldn't do anything but stand there, frozen in the moment. Consumed by fear at first, a few seconds passed when the dread quickly pivoted back to the sense of protection, the same feeling she felt at the graves. She continued standing there, allowing a few moments to pass before beginning her journey back to the house. She was in hopes that whoever this visitor was would stay nearby. Realizing the lateness of the day, she picked up her pace as it was time to start preparing food. She knew if dinner wasn't ready when Edgar called for it, she would be physically reminded of her obligations. Beatrice quietly approached a hen at the edge of the garden; when close enough, she leaped at the chicken, picking it up in one swift move. Wringing the chicken's neck, she began preparing the bird for dinner. As she scrubbed the hen, she heard Edgar yell for her from the half-rotted screen door facing the garden. He watched her clean the feathers from the bird with fierce intensity, shaking his head before yelling out at his daughter.

"Sometimes I feel like doing that to you!"

As she looked at him with a stare, almost daring him to try, he began to laugh.

"I'm headed to the City—be back day after tomorrow."

Beatrice stopped scouring the bird, maintaining her stance perfectly still, almost in a rebellious position. She was not concerned about the threat her father made; she was accustomed to his intimidating demeanor. She was, however, taken aback as he was leaving her alone for an extended period; this had never happened before. She recalled the man in the woods, the gravestones being cleared, her body altering, and Edgar leaving for more than a few hours. Were these indicators suggesting a change in her future?

It was oddly quiet and lonesome being in the house by herself while she prepared the chicken for her dinner. If Edgar wasn't eating or sleeping, he was rarely in the house. Knowing he was close provided an odd sense of comfort to her. She didn't like her dad and longed for the day when she wouldn't be near him anymore, yet there was a longing for his company which confused Beatrice. How could she have no emotions for him when he was around yet missed him, knowing he wasn't home? She became mindful of this odd emotion and sought to better understand it. Her sleep was intermittent that night as she kept wondering who the man she saw in the woods was. It seemed as if he belonged, but why?

"Who could that have been?"

Finally, she concluded it must be her protector in life, and with that thought, she finally slept. She awoke to the rooster crowing and realized she was late for her chores. As she moved to the edge of the bed, she stood up and felt something wet trickling down her leg. She looked over her shoulder to see the bed was colored and moist as if she had soiled herself in the night. She raised her dress to find her underclothes stained a reddish-brown color, left by ovarian secretions resembling blood. Without a female in her life to explain what was happening, she had no clue what this blood was or what was happening to her, much less what to do. She began to panic, thinking she might bleed to death while her dad was gone. It only took a few seconds for her to realize he wouldn't have helped anyway. A knock on the door startled her, and she began to sob out loud.

Between the tears, she called out.

"Who is it?"

"Sheriff Turner. Everything all right in there?"

"Help me!"

Those words would be the last thing Beatrice was aware of for the next several hours. When she awoke, she was back in her bed. Her bedding had been changed, and she was dressed in a clean nightgown. A beautiful blond-haired woman with curls gently pinned on top of her head sat in the corner chair, working her needlepoint. A mature woman, middle-aged from Beatrice's point of view, very poised and very well-pressed. Beatrice knew this woman but couldn't come to terms as to why. In her weakened, barely awake state, her first thought was that she was dying, and the woman was her momma waiting to collect her. Finally, the figure looked up from her craft, studying Beatrice for a moment before speaking.

"There, there, dear. You are all right. You've had quite a fright this morning."

The memories of her bathing Beatrice and dressing her in her first dress just days after her momma died came flooding back.

"Who are you?" Beatrice asked.

"I'm the Sheriff's wife, dear. Do you remember me?"

She remembered the kindness this woman had provided to her.

"My precious young girl, you are becoming a woman. Do you know what I am talking about?"

Beatrice shook her head no.

The Sheriff's wife explained in detail the happenings to a woman's body when she is able to become pregnant. She spent a long time talking about required hygiene and told Beatrice how to calculate when this time would repeat its process. She told Beatrice not to be afraid, this was just a part of life, and at some point in time, it would go away. She went into detail about feelings and desires that would confuse her and to be careful around certain men as they would try to take advantage of her now that she was a woman. Beatrice asked the woman to explain what she meant. As she began to talk, the Sheriff entered the house and told his wife it was time to go. He had a radio call requiring him to return to the station as quickly as possible. He told Beatrice to rest and let her know the eggs from the chickens had been collected and that he picked the ripe vegetables as well, all on the table in the main room. Beatrice couldn't help herself; she slowly, but with purpose, crawled out of bed and ran to the man, and hugged him. She held him so tight he felt as if he might lose his breath.

"Please take me away from here," she begged.

The Sheriff explained that he didn't have cause to take her, but should there ever be a reason he could legally take her away, he would. Beatrice told him about the graves being cleared and the man she saw running through the woods. The Sheriff and his wife stared at each other in disbelief; could it have been? They assured Beatrice the man wouldn't ever hurt her and doubted he would ever return.

It was not long after the Sheriff and his wife left the shack that Edgar returned from the City; Beatrice decided it best to not mention anything about the Sheriff's visit or her becoming a woman. She feared that her father would be one of those men who would take advantage of her, as the Sheriff's wife had warned. She had seen her dad abusing a girl in the main room of the shack on occasion. He thought Beatrice to be asleep and that she wouldn't see the two of them. Beatrice assumed this was what the Sheriff's wife was talking about. The woman came around the farm every so often, and each time Edgar would abuse her again. Beatrice didn't understand why this woman wanted him to hurt her. The sounds she made were awful, moaning and screaming. Even when she would scratch or hit Edgar, they would keep at it until she finally stopped making noises. Recalling once the woman squealed so loud and then immediately after went silent, Beatrice thought the woman to be dead.

A few weeks more passed before Edgar left the farm again. On this trip, he didn't load any of his liquor and dressed like he was going to church, a place she was sure he had never set foot in. When Edgar returned late that evening, Leroy was with him, fresh from prison. Leroy had vague memories of his little sister and ignored her when exiting the truck; he showed no concern she was there. Making his way past her towards the home he had been taken from, Beatrice observed him, noting how prison had hardened him. He had numerous scars on his face and hands, the result of the betrayals he perpetrated while serving his time. Men in the prison believed he to be the one providing information on the whereabouts of their illegal businesses, and he paid dearly for their assumptions. His eyes were black with anger. His skin was leathery from being in the sun too long, his hair blonde and unkempt. His body was muscular and lean; she could only assume it was from the hard labor he had to perform. Dressed in blue jeans cinched tight around his waist, a clean white undershirt covered by a new white dress shirt, both neatly tucked into his pants. His ensemble was completed by shiny new shoes, looking as if they had just left the box. What teeth he had remaining were yellowed and stained.

Beatrice surmised the fresh new clothes must have been issued by the prison; she couldn't imagine her father spending any money on anyone, including his only living son.

Leroy stood on the front porch of the shack looking around the farm, his eye landing on the rotting plow; he commented on how not much had changed. He lit a cigarette while proceeding down the steps to the yard; looking back through the screen door, he asked Edgar where the hooch was. He stared at Beatrice while waiting for an answer. She knew where the stills were but would never confess that information in front of her father. She turned her gaze towards the door her father had walked through; Edgar shouted out from beside the door.

"The booze isn't allowed in here. There should never be evidence of anything illegal in the house due to the nosy Sheriff coming around asking questions. You can drink in the barns or sheds when you ain't working".

Mumbling an OK, Leroy walked away. Edgar exited the house through the screen door to follow his son, who was headed straight for the barns. After observing the familial interaction, Beatrice knew deep down in her soul she must be very cautious around her brother. The question had been answered why her dad wanted his boy home to help produce liquor. In the first few weeks of being home, he did little beyond lifting a jug to drink until he couldn't stand up, often falling to the ground and passing out. His drunken state led to physical cruelties imposed on Beatrice. Once when he fell down in his drunken state, he hit her just because she was too close to him. Another time she thought he was asleep and was looking at him; he opened his eyes and slapped her for the act of curiosity.

Leroy only slowed his drinking after being threatened by his father. It was made known if he didn't sober up enough to work, he would have to leave the farm and possibly go back to prison. The memories of his last years in jail provided enough fear for Leroy to only drink after work was done. His father ordered him to limit consumption to one jug after work was completed daily.

Leroy learned something new every day on how to operate the stills; the correct boiling point, the proper mixture of grain for the most potent product, and how much wood was required to create enough heat for distillation. Every nuance required to make the best product they could. They must constantly produce with a consistent quality, or else their customers would cause them unnecessary grief. As Leroy learned the craft, he became proficient in running the vats, leaving Edgar free to make more runs to the clubs in and around Oklahoma City. Edgar was happy with this arrangement; Leroy did not want to be around people, and Edgar was longing to have some fun. As long as Beatrice managed the care of the farm and fed them, everyone was content, and she was left alone. Should dinner be late or not cooked to fit their taste buds, she would be whipped with a belt, verbally scolded, and forced to make something else to eat.

Over the next few months, Beatrice fully developed into a young woman. She worked harder than ever to stay out of sight and away from the two men in her life. With no one to lean on and the Sheriff's visits happening less often, she decided she should soon run away to find a better life. Beatrice closely followed the Sheriff's wife's advice for keeping herself clean during and after her cycle. Awaking early one morning to her course beginning, she quietly retreated to the creek to avoid any chance of her brother knowing where she was. Reaching the bank, she disrobed before slowly wading into the stream. Before applying the lye soap to cleanse her body, she wanted to enjoy the fresh water on her skin. Soaking in the refreshing river somehow renewed her soul. After several minutes of relaxing in the stream, she washed her undergarments and tattered dress, laying them out on the rocks to dry. As the clothes released the river's water into the air, she reclined on the river's edge to enjoy the warm sun.

While she lay there, she sensed someone nearby, watching her. The first thought to come to mind was her protector was watching over her. As she peered up and down the river, she spotted Leroy standing tall on a rock, his pants unbuttoned and hanging loosely on his buttocks. With his semi-erect manhood in his hand, he observed her thin, shapely, naked frame lying in the sun. Massaging his growing member with one hand, he stroked his muscular chest with the other. At first, she wasn't sure what he was doing or if he indeed knew she could see him. Having seen a few bulls and studs, she knew his hardened member's sexual excitement. She didn't understand this activity when no one else was around; the sight was very confusing to her. Leroy knew he would catch hell for this if she told anyone, but he continued looking her up and down while he managed the task at hand. He reckoned there was no one to be told, so he would just finish pleasuring himself while he ogled her young fresh body. Beatrice quickly gathered up her partially dried clothes, heading out of sight to dress. Just before she was out of sight from Leroy, Beatrice heard him release a loud grunt. She stopped and turned to see if he had perhaps fallen into the river; she instead saw him smiling at her as he released his semen into the water.

That night, after dinner, Edgar left for the City for his rounds; Leroy beat Beatrice with his belt until she promised never to tell a soul what she witnessed that day.

"I have needs, goddamnit, and I can't do anything about them because of your damn father!"

This scared Beatrice; at that moment, she understood what the Sheriff's wife had warned her about. From that moment on, Beatrice did all she could to avoid Leroy, no matter what. She would not allow sleep to begin until she was sure he was solidly slumbering; most nights, she laid awake in the dark of her bed, fearing he was coming for her.

This ongoing lack of rest brought Beatrice to exhaustion; her abilities to function normally were at a minimum. Each night she yearned for sleep in hopes of recovery. It had been several weeks since the incident at the river had occurred, and even though Leroy spent most of his time in the sheds, Beatrice steered clear of her brother. He rarely came to the house for anything, including sleep.

Delivery day came quickly once again; following the norm when going into town, Leroy loaded up the truck with crates of bottled spirits. As her father prepared to leave that night, Beatrice saw Leroy head back to the stills. In her exhausted state, she decided she was safe to lay down and attempt some sleep, even with Edgar heading into town.

Leroy had grown tired of his self-pleasuring, missing the warmth of another being to satisfy him. During his incarceration, he learned many ways to pleasure the flesh; he was hungry to feel warm wet flesh around his manhood.

His arousal that evening led him back to the house; he looked through the window observing Beatrice in her bed. His animal instinct engaged, and his primal desire became a guide to find satisfaction. Believing her to be asleep, he disrobed while standing on the porch. Standing there naked, he breathed in the night air; then he raised the jug he'd been drinking from to his lips for another sip. The intense liquor warmed his insides as the cool air around his body stimulated his genitals. The excitement of what he was preparing to do caused him to grow bigger and harder than he had ever known. He entered the house, standing by the table where he could see her sleeping; he began tugging at his hard member. Once more, the jug reached his lips, the last bit of liquid consumed in one gulp. With that drink, he sat the vessel on the table and entered the room where Beatrice slept. Covering her mouth to minimize the noise, he mounted her relaxed body. Awakening to the pain of being penetrated unexpectedly, she reacted in fear, contorting her body in every direction in an attempt to escape. He pulled his hand back high in the air and struck her across the face. So fiercely she could hear the echo around the room of the bones in her face being crushed. The more she screamed, the more furious he became, his growing rage causing his thrust to be stronger each time. Her screams moved to sobs of agony as he climaxed.

"Bitch—you're my whore now, fuuuuuuck."

With his anger and seed released, he stopped moving, remaining on top of her, keeping her pinned to the bed. His heavy breathing lasted for what seemed like an eternity. The blood from her facial wound flowed down her cheek, joining the blood on the bed from her stolen virginity. Pulling out of her, he stood up, making himself very tall and proud, satisfied with his manly ability to take what he wanted. He threatened her to never speak of this moment.

"I will be back for more."

After the beatings she received from the river incident, she knew she mustn't ever speak of this.

Leaving the house, he grabbed his clothes from the porch, strolled naked across the land, and returned to his chosen home in the sheds. Beatrice crawled onto the floor and cried from the pain of being ripped open, both physically and emotionally. The broken cheekbone emitted horrible throbs of pain, but nothing compared to the emotional tear in her soul. A cut deeper than any knife could wield, a wound invisible to the eye. As she lay there in her emotional and physical agony, she realized she must find a way to leave before he retook her. She knew so little of the world and its cruelties but knew without question she was not meant to be treated this way. She must find a way to escape.

She begged a higher power to help her, and her focus turned to her brothers, long gone. Maybe they could help her from where they were. She asked the gods to give her direction so she might have a better life beyond agony and descent.

Drawn back to the graves where her mother and siblings were buried, she left the house ambling towards the path she had taken so many times before. Her nightgown torn and bloodied, her body weak from the trauma, her mind reeling from what had just happened. Her walk through the woods was somehow different; she didn't feel alone. She had an intense sensation that new beginnings were just around the corner.

It would be three months before she understood the implications of this moment in time.

Chapter 6

Thadeus began to see a change in Mary. He wasn't quite sure of the origin driving the new spirit he observed in her but was happy to see she appeared more relaxed and, indeed, more pleasant to be around. Something was also changing in him, something he had never felt before, a need he had never noticed. Perhaps it was his age; maybe he was growing tired from the constant need to be on point; whatever the reason, he was becoming increasingly aware he wanted something more. Thadeus had managed his life and appearance to ensure he was considered a ladies' man; his work and life away from home benefitted from his endless charm. As a result of his way of being, he was forced to live his life as far removed from Mary as possible. Both of their needs were met by various means, hers within her home and his by outside alliances. Thadeus somewhat thought he understood Mary and ensured he was always proper with her. Occasionally, he would shout at her for a random act he might disagree with, but he never hit her. From various conversations, he knew just enough of her past to know physical abuse was common in her upbringing. Even though they were never intimate, he consciously chose not to reopen past wounds from within her. He had begun to question if finding intimacy in their awkward relationship might somehow fulfill both of them.

Thadeus, alongside his business partners, ran the joints in Oklahoma City. He had personally established a few other places around the state, which he ran independently of his business partners. He utilized his social skillset and various means of persuasion to amass a sizable amount of cash, untaxed and unknown to the government. Using connections that had the power to move mountains when he requested it, life was easy. Between a senator, a couple of judges, both state and local, and several sheriff's offices, he could resolve most situations with a simple, usually verbal, request. His reputation was one of being able to maneuver and persuade people, perhaps even coerce them, rarely relying on violence to accomplish what he wanted. In a time when a gun most easily resolved challenges, his use of alternative methods eliminated the burden of disposing of someone who might be disagreeable. By understanding his business associates, he created a tit-for-tat system, a structure where everyone got what they needed. His reputation preceded him; he was known for robbing banks where no carnage was left in his wake. People walked away from participating in one of his heists, happy they encountered him and his troop, as it gave them a story to tell. He was, oddly, a bit of a folk hero.

His nom de plume, if you will, was Pretty Man. He was tall and handsome at six foot three, with a perfect thirty-six-inch waist and forty-two-inch chest. A frame that lent itself to fantasy. Jet black hair with simple tossed curls, all managed and forced into place with Brylcreem. Eyes the color of the water near a beach, light and practically see-through. So piercing that whoever peered into them was momentarily beguiled. His cheekbones were high and pronounced, with lips so perfectly carved above his cleft chin they begged to be kissed. His only physical flaw was a small scar to the left of his nose, high on his cheek, just below his eye; barely noticeable but prominent enough to make him appear rugged. He was always charming to the ladies and a man that most men wanted to be. Always dressed to perfection, thanks to his wife's efforts. He lived the life most people envied and was having fun doing it. He broke almost every law and never received any punishment. One must understand it is a matter of perspective; he was safe as long as he had the right connections and dirty laundry on those who might convict him. Generally speaking, if fear of being outed for some dirty deed wasn't enough reason, an anonymous bag of cash would forgive most sins. Most everyone in town and around Oklahoma knew who Pretty Man was, except Mary. She had heard tales of this legendary figure and read about him in the paper but never knew he was her husband. Thadeus, A.K.A. Pretty Man, managed never to be photographed with his face showing. This anonymity allowed him great benefits, and his liaisons liked that he was elusive. It provided sanctuary for them as well.

On a rare occasion, Thadeus would venture out of the City to Carter County to visit one of his speakeasies. The young Sheriff in Carter County was a stubborn goat and was not one willing to be bought. The Sheriff believed in the law and made it clear to Thadeus that as long as he kept things quiet, he would stay out of the way. He didn't want anything from Thadeus; not money, not favors, nothing. Thadeus often questioned this allowance, considering how stoic the Sheriff appeared. He decided it best to not question the motives of the Sheriff as long as his business was making money and no trouble was had.

It had been around seven years since he and Edgar had first met; it was at this gathering he experienced the quality of whiskey produced at the Farrell distillery. Shortly after that introduction, he decided to open his first joint in Ardmore. The previous Sheriff died during a sting looking for illegal production facilities, leaving the young deputy to take over. Thadeus speculated the young Sheriff was aware that the barns holding the best hooch in the state lay just outside this little town, within his county. With that interpretation of the Sheriff's knowledge, Thadeus made every effort to keep a very low profile when dealing with Edgar.

It was still relatively hot in September 1936 when Thadeus took a trip south of the City. The summer had run long, keeping the fall season at bay. Thadeus sensed a change was about to occur; this made him uneasy. A slight smell of fall was in the air, the leaves turning orange, plum, and yellow, began to appear all around him. Even with the leaves altering their color, the heat from summer persisted. Thadeus made the drive from Oklahoma City south to Ardmore in record time. He slowly pulled into the dirt lot next to his place of business, parking the mile-long Chrysler just shy of the rubbish bin. He sat in the meticulous white vinyl interior for a moment, taking in his surroundings and pondering life, wondering why he felt anxious. His nerve endings tingled, his body tense; he sensed something was about to happen. Perhaps it was merely his anticipation of the change of seasons. As he opened the door of the car, he noticed a minute spec of mud on his shoe. It was just a smudge, but it made him question how Mary would have missed it. She was always so focused on everything being clean and precise. While staring at the dirt residing on his shoe, deep in thought, he heard a man nearby clear his throat. Thadeus was slow to react; in his line of business, a quick reaction could be the difference between dead or alive. He casually looked up to find the Sheriff standing beside the open car door.

"Morning, Sheriff Turner. Keeping things quiet down here?"

The Sheriff stood quietly for a moment before responding,

"Yes, Sir, Mr. Johnson. Hasn't been a bank robbery in my county since I took over."

Thadeus knew this was an attempt to rile him up. Being the politician he was, he smiled.

"That's great news. Let's keep on doing what we are doing, and that record should be maintained."

Sheriff Turner inquired in a soft but direct tone.

"What brings you down to our quiet little part of the state?"

Due to his years around the county, he was fully aware of why Pretty Man made visits to his town. The young Sheriff kept an eye on the drinking establishment, constantly monitoring who came and went. As long as there was no trouble coming out of there, he remained a mere observer, never interrupting.

"Headed over to see a man on Honey Creek."

Thadeus immediately noticed the Sheriff's eye shoot up as his posture straightened; this gave him pause. He wondered why the unusual and quick reaction from the lawman.

When checking on his business interests in Ardmore, Thadeus rarely visited Edgar's place. On occasion, when production didn't keep up with demand, he would drive out to the farm and have a direct face-to-face conversation with Edgar. On this particular visit, Thadeus intended to advise Edgar that business was growing beyond expectations. He needed to know what Edgar was willing to do to increase output in order to meet supply requirements. He would inform Edgar that other suppliers would be brought into the fold if he couldn't find a solution to ensure on-time deliveries. Thadeus' goal was to keep customers content, thereby avoiding complaints about the quality of his establishment.

"Be safe over there, Mr. Johnson; you know the oldest boy is out of prison and back home now. He has a bit of a temper, I've heard. Rumor has it he isn't allowed in the local watering hole after some incident that happened recently. But that's all just rumor—"

Sheriff Turner stopped himself mid-sentence, realizing Thadeus' cold blue eyes were staring right through him.

Thadeus was taking in the information, processing the warning along with the perceived implication. He still wasn't clear why the Sheriff was turning a blind eye to his bar or Edgar's business. He wondered about the young Sheriff's motives, what secrets this man carried through life.

Deciding it best to move on before anything else was said, he spoke,

"Good day, Sheriff Turner; you take care now."

Thadeus's tone was very soft and gentle, employing one of his manipulation tactics used to throw people off.

"Sure, will do. Let me know if there is any trouble out on Honey Creek that needs my attention."

The two men nodded to each other while tipping their hats and then moved on with their business. Each now knowing they had a need for the other more significant than either wanted to acknowledge. Thadeus realized the Sheriff's cooperation to let the business run was necessary, and Sheriff Turner needed to keep the farm on Honey Creek anonymous for Beatrice's sake. One phone call to the Feds and the distillery would be eliminated in an instant; that would be a situation neither of these men could afford. Thadeus knew about the incident some years back when Edgar's place was raided during prohibition but never knew who disclosed the location of the farm. It had been speculated that the son in prison made a deal with the state to get away from his father; this didn't make sense as he served a lengthy sentence. It was neither here nor there; time passed, and laws changed; it was now legal to sell booze provided you paid your taxes. Thadeus realized it was risky to avoid the tax collectors but felt compelled to do so. He felt giving up his hard-earned cash was simply unacceptable.

The Sheriff was concerned about why Pretty Man was headed to the Farrell farm. He feared what would happen to Beatrice if the booze stopped flowing from Honey Creek. Pondering various scenarios for her, he kept forefront in his mind the promise made to his lover so long ago.

Thadeus made the drive through the rolling hills to visit Edgar. He found the trip that day most relaxing, the blacktop road winding through the magnificent endless trees, the wind blowing around him. The mud on his shoe continued to creep into his thoughts, nagging at him. He made the turn onto the unmarked driveway leading to Edgar's place, his thoughts moving from the dirty shoe to his conversation with the Sheriff. What warning was the Sheriff delivering with his statement to "Be safe over there." Thadeus didn't know where the booze was made and was personally glad not to bear that secret. When visiting Edgar, it was always a game of chance if he would be home; he would wait if necessary this time. As he approached the dilapidated house, he observed the weathered paint peeled away from its surface, the aged wood exposed, slowly rotting due to neglect. Seeing the windows cracked and dirty from seemingly never having been washed, he was puzzled as to where Edgar spent the money he made. Looking around the farm, one could easily conclude the people who lived here were barely able to survive. The hefty amount of cash Thadeus paid Edgar for each delivery suggested this was all a facade to keep people from asking questions. From his time spent around people who consumed spirits, Thadeus had learned customers who thought someone had too much money were inclined to beg or steal from him. Secrecy in this business was a better part of valor. Secrecy was a powerful tool used abundantly by both Edgar and Thadeus.

Good fortune smiled on Thadeus that day, for Edgar was home sitting on his porch, gearing up for a busy evening. Edgar heard the car come off the county highway, whirring down the dirt road towards him. Not expecting any visitors, he figured it to be the nosy Sheriff causing him grief for no reason. Edgar sat in his rocking chair, gently moving to and fro, patiently watching for the car to appear in the clearing at the end of the driveway. He was surprised to see the long sleek car arrive and yet even more surprised when Thadeus stepped out of the driver's seat. Edgar didn't care for the man showing up at his home uninvited and unannounced but knew he must be gracious to his largest customer. Walking down the steps and across the dirt, he forced an amiable smile before engaging in conversation. After a moment of small talk, Thadeus got straight to the point he needed to make clear: production had to pick up, or business would be moved. Edgar was not happy hearing this threat and responded in kind. Should Thadeus or his partners choose to alter the delivery schedules or reduce demand, Edgar would have Leroy visit Thadeus to "work things out." Edgar was confident in his product; he felt he could afford to be a bully. He believed the customers needed him more than he needed them. Edgar's arrogance triggered Thadeus; he didn't like being threatened. It was not his way of doing business, although he knew how to manage a ruffian when necessary.

Thadeus stood very still and non-responsive as Edgar spewed his threats. When Edgar was done speaking, Thadeus stood his ground, making it clear this was bigger than the two of them. Thadeus casually explained to Edgar,

"If you want to stay out of jail, you should just comply and increase production."

Thadeus retreated to his car, walking softly, listening for any possible peril approaching from behind him. He settled into the front seat, pulling the door closed, he noticed a young girl standing by the edge of the porch. Questioning if she had been there the entire time, he continued assessing her, making out her beautiful, natural features. She was tall, blonde, and very fit. He was taken aback to see this young girl living here, as he only knew of the one bastard child. He focused on turning the car around in the dirt patch while paying close attention to Edgar. He assessed Edgar was processing his threat of jail and attempting to determine if it had merit. When he looked back to where the young girl had stood, she was gone. Perhaps she had been a mirage; he quickly dismissed that thought as her image was a clear photograph imprinted in his mind's eye.

The road home seemed long and the drive monotonous as he returned to Oklahoma City. He was becoming melancholy, thinking of the young mirage girl, wondering how Mary had missed cleaning the mud on his shoe, pondering why the Sheriff was being overly forgiving. If one didn't know better, they might have assumed he was developing a conscience.

He arrived home very late that night; closing the car door gingerly, he entered the house through the side kitchen door. He quietly undressed, relieved himself, and crawled into bed. He assumed Mary would be upset with him for missing dinner, but he would deal with that should it arise. As he lay there next to his wife, he thought back on the day reconciling he should have told her he would be out of pocket that evening, but it hadn't crossed his mind. He promised himself he would make it up to her tomorrow, and with that thought, he was quickly asleep.

He arose the next morning to the aroma of fresh coffee and the smell of bacon in the frying pan. Mary had long been up cleaning the house, preparing for her usual busy day ahead. He entered the kitchen, expecting growling and hissing; Mary quietly turned to him and smiled.

"Coffee?"

He was thankful for this and glad to see her smiling. Whatever was going on with her was a wonder; still curious about the changes, he began to see her in a different light. Emotions, which had never existed in this house, had started to emerge. Mary placed his breakfast consisting of fresh bacon and fried eggs, in front of him while gently arranging the silverware on the table. She did not sit with him that morning like she usually did; only a single meal had been prepared. Lightly kissing his forehead, Mary returned to the counter, where she used a dishtowel to make a final sweep across the white ceramic tile, gently pushing the crumbs into her hands. Smiling, she dropped them in the waste can as she exited the room. This sequence of events caught him by surprise; this was entirely out of character for her. He ate in silence, continuing to wonder what was happening around him. Returning to the kitchen after Thadeus had finished his breakfast, she smiled at him while removing the soiled dishes from the table.

Placing them next to the sink after she scraped every last bit of food off the plate into the trash. She diligently began her obsessive cleaning practice. After she wiped the plate clean in the trash bin, she rinsed it thoroughly with scalding water and scrubbed it with soap and a Brillo pad. Rinsed a second time, scrubbed with additional soap using the opposite side of the pad, and a final rinse in scalding water before drying. Next were the saucer and cup, both following the same ritual. While she worked through her routine of washing the dinnerware and utensils one at a time, she quietly hummed a little tune.

This routine was the same as the day before; from his perspective, this was her norm, except for the humming. He had never heard a musical note come from her during their years of marriage. She seemed somewhat free for a change; although the obsessive cleaning was the same, something was different. Another surprise for Thadeus, yet one more shift in behavior, creating a higher level of concern for him. What had changed in her? What had he not noticed? Where was this newfound appreciation of life coming from? He knew the obvious choice for most women would be that a baby was on the way, but as she had confessed long ago she was sterile and they didn't have sexual relations, he was confident that was not the case. For a brief moment, he questioned if there was another man but quickly put that thought away as he knew she didn't like to be touched and was never naked in front of anyone. He often suspected she didn't even look at herself in the mirror prior to dressing. This odd puritanical behavior had existed way before the day they wed.

She finished her tasks, putting things away before removing her apron and placing it on its hook. She walked passed the kitchen table into the living room to retrieve her purse and gloves. Mary returned to the kitchen table and looked her husband in the eye.

"Your clothes are pressed and hanging on your valet. I have an appointment in town and must leave now to catch the bus. Have a splendid day. Will I see you for dinner tonight?"

"Absolutely. May I drive you to your appointment?"

This was a shock to Mary as her husband had never offered to drive her anywhere.

Mary carefully composed herself.

"No, thank you."

Thadeus caught the shock in her eyes and became suspicious of her actions. With the polite exchange of goodbyes, Mary left the house through the front door, hurriedly walking to the bus stop. She was not late for the bus but felt compelled to move away from him as quickly as possible.

Thadeus promptly dressed and made his way to the Chrysler. As he was a master of being stealthy, he followed the bus Mary was on without her ever seeing him. Every few minutes, she would look over her shoulder for him, but the car she refused to learn to drive never came into view. She believed she had managed to avoid the impending conflict one more day. Arriving at her stop in Moore, Mary exited the bus looking in every direction to be sure her husband had not followed her. Feeling confident she was alone, she crossed and walked up the street, her gait prancing with a lilt in her step. Entering the shop, she heard the familiar clanging of the bell on the door; this always calmed her. The sound of the doorbell represented freedom to her; she had grown very fond of the simple, high-pitched ding ringing out each time the door was opened. It was a symbol reminding her she was gaining control of her life. Carefully and quickly, she put away her belongings, greeted her loving employer, and began to work. Focused on her work, she quickly lost track of her surroundings and of time itself. Busily sewing hems, pleats, repairing zippers, letting out a dress for a woman who couldn't resist dessert. Intensely focused on her work, she heard the front doorbell ring again. A customer had entered the shop.

Lottie Bell called from the back of the shop,

"Mary, would you take care of the customer, please."

Mary finished stitching the dress seam, completing the garment. Lifting the foot feed and snipping the thread, she removed the dress from the sewing machine. Laying it gently aside, she rose from the sewing table. Bumping into the work table directly behind her, she knocked over a small blotter of ink, splattering the contents onto her skirt. Usually, this would have sent Mary into hysteria, but as she assessed the mess, she looked up to see him; Thadeus was standing in the doorway. The ink stain became the least of her concerns. Quickly setting the jar upright, she rushed to the front of the shop. Quietly she begged Thadeus not to make a scene; she asked that they discuss the matter later at home. He recognized the panicked look on her face he had seen many times before and made the conscious decision they would deal with this right then and there. He began shouting at her with a contemptuous tone; on and on, he bombarded her with questions about why she was there and what she was doing. The loud raucous in the shop quickly brought Lottie Bell and Herbert to the front of the store.

Witnessing the man shouting at Mary, the shop owners stood there wondering why he was yelling at her. Thadeus finally noticed them in the background and composed himself; it was then he was greeted by Herbert and Lottie Bell like old friends. This caught Mary entirely by surprise. Why would her employer know her husband? They were so far out from town she had made sure to keep a long distance between home and work to avoid this happening.

Herbert was the first to respond.

"I didn't expect to see you in my shop!"

Thadeus turned to Herbert, his face red with fury.

"I didn't know you had my wife working here!"

Mary shouted at her husband to leave and assured him they would discuss this at home. The response returned from her husband's mouth was harsh and robust; he demanded she retrieve her purse and leave with him that instant. Having known Thadeus for some time, Herbert suggested he go on about his day; he would see to it that Mary got home on time.

"Give it a little time to cool off before you say something you wish you hadn't, son."

Lottie Bell quickly deflected the situation by taking Mary to the back to treat the stain on her skirt.

"You go on now; we need to clean this up. She can't go out in public with this nasty stain on her dress! Go on now—Go ON!"

Lottie Bell could be very powerful and demanding; her tone and aggressive behavior caused Thadeus to pause and Herbert to laugh a deep, hearty guffaw.

As he turned to go, Thadeus looked at his wife.

"I'm disappointed you would lie to me. I need to understand the change in you."

He spoke this with a kindness Mary had never heard from him. She knew very little about this man she had married; his knowledge of her was at par. Both of them completely unable to see beyond their own selfish needs.

Lottie Bell coerced Mary to the dressing room, where she gently unzipped Mary's skirt, letting it fall to the floor. As she began to loosen the stained petticoat, Mary began to cry. At first, only a few small tears, then larger drops fell from her red-swelling eyes, all this leading to uncontrollable sobbing. Lottie Bell assumed the waterworks to be a result of the emotional outburst that had just occurred. She knew Mary had secrets; she had known many women with the same habits as Mary and was keenly aware of the reasons behind their peculiar actions. She pulled Mary close to her bosom, holding her tightly while Mary released a wave of sadness induced by her husband's soft words. Herbert entered the room and was immediately dismissed. Lottie Bell informed him he should go out front or around back; he couldn't be there. After several minutes of emotional release, the sobs subsided to quiet sniffles. Mary was, for the moment, all cried out. Lottie Bell released her friend from the bear hug, gently wiping the tears away from Mary's mascara-stained face. Mary carried a great deal of shame for so many things in her past; this was just another layer of embarrassment added on. Before Mary could stop her, her loving boss released the petticoat, letting it fall to the floor. Upon its release from her body, Mary's eyes popped wide open as Lottie Bell let out a scream filled with horror. Even though he had been banished, Herbert ran into the room to find out what the screams were about, stopping immediately upon seeing Mary's scarred body.

"My God, what have they done to you girl? Who did this to you?"

Mary could no longer hide the multiple scars on her body.

Her reply came in a childlike shy voice,

"Mother did."

Chapter 7

Bettie followed her morning routine of breakfast, bible study, washing, and drying dishes. Putting the melamine dinnerware immediately away in the cupboard, she moved on to removing food from the freezer for that evening's meal. All this occurring in conjunction with her mentally preparing for her trip to visit Mary at the hospital. She began waxing sentimental about the life she had lived. The years since the divorce from her husband had been tough. The decision to leave and start anew had been her choice. She believed this was the best way to move forward out of a relationship full of anger and despair. As a result of her daily visits with Mary, she began to question the choice. Her perspective of her former mother-in-law had changed over the past few weeks. Seeing the agony endured by Mary, the pain suffered during the first round of cancer, and now repeating the fight to no avail caused Bettie to question many of the choices she had made in her life. She realized she was guilty of making snap judgments, not taking time to know the reasons why people acted out.

Bettie never sought to understand how one's own reality developed or molded their behavior. While quietly brushing her hair that morning before leaving, she thought about Mary's strength and drive to keep going. Laying her brush down on her dresser, she began a prayer of thanks for this woman in her life, a thoughtful meditation lasting the entire drive to the downtown hospital. Spending time in contemplative prayer forced her to slow down and observe the people around her. People she selfishly never gave the time to take notice of before.

The limestone hospital building, which would be Mary's last home, sat on top of a divine, gently rising hill. Wooden benches selectively situated under large oak trees on the perfectly manicured lawn led the way to the entrance. Two stone water fountains sat on each side of the front veranda, providing a soothing cascade of sound as one passed by. If one looked to the right from the doors, beyond the water features, the beautiful slow-moving river crossing the flat prairie land was visible, just beyond the edge of the hospital boundaries. The rich, fertile soil flowed from the waterfalls down to the river's edge. On the other side of the water, the flatlands filled with native grasses, perfect for feeding cattle, began. As Bettie walked past the benches under the oak trees, strolling towards the sliding double doors into the hospital, she was reminded of a quote she had recently read in her bible study material.

"Life without hills to climb leaves one without an appreciation of when walking is effortless."

Arriving on the oncology floor, Bettie exited the elevator to be met by one of the nurses attending to Mary. She asked Bettie to wait in the chairs by the nurses' station.

The nurse informed Bettie that the doctor had just left the room, and the news was not good. She went on to inform Bettie that John Edward needed a few moments to confirm his mother's do not resuscitate wishes. The nurse gently patted Bettie on the shoulder and smiled sweetly.

Bettie's eyes began to swell with emotion; she looked around to find a diversion to focus on. Her eyes landed on the bag hanging from the IV stand the nurse was holding onto.

"At this point, there's not much left to do but maintain comfort."

The plastic bag was filled with morphine; Mary Bennet's name was on the label.

A few minutes passed before John Edward stepped out of the room to find Bettie.

"She is wanting to know where you are."

Bettie smiled and confessed to seeing the morphine bag and assumed they were focusing on comfort versus treatment. John Edward shook his head, affirming her statement, and asked her to please go and visit.

"According to what the doctors are telling me, she will become less lucid every day until she finally just goes to sleep. We have to make the most of the time we have now. I am thankful that you are here for her. She seems hell-bent on spending time alone with you."

John Edward was curious as to what they were talking about, but something deep inside told him not to pry. He and his ex-wife had not had a meaningful discussion in the past ten years; surely she would tell him if his mother wanted him to know something that pertained to him.

Bettie gently touched him on the elbow, acknowledging his pain with a simple smile before speaking.

"Go home and get some rest. I'll be here until around 3:30."

Bettie walked the long hallway peering into other rooms, wondering who else on this floor had been told their time on this earth was nearly over. She stopped short of Mary's door, summoning that good old Southern charm into service. Taking a deep breath while pushing the door open, she entered the room. The giant faux smile on Bettie's face did not fool the woman lying in bed.

Mary looked straight into her eyes.

"You never could hide anything; I see it in your eyes; you know I'm done for!"

The smile slid from her lips as she genuinely felt sorry for this woman. Bettie remembered a time, some twelve years back, when Mary had the double mastectomy, being assured by the doctors all the cancer had been removed from her. Yet here they were, once again, fighting the dreadful disease, and this time with minimal hope for recovery.

Lost time never to be reclaimed.

"Bettie, I don't blame you for your divorce. I know you think I do, but I don't. In many ways, I am an old, bitter woman; I own that. I made choices long ago that seemed the right thing at the time. This long life I have lived has contained more bitter than good. It is important I leave this earth with a few things cleared up. I cannot tell John Edward what I am about to tell you. He must never know how I stole the most valuable gift in the world because of my and Thadeus' selfishness. I need to make peace on this earth for the next life."

Mary was beginning to slightly slur her words as she spoke. The morphine coursing through her veins was beginning to do its job.

"I was once so young and free, without a care in the world. Life was very promising and without complication before my Dad died when I was nine. Life was gay and full of music and dancing, grand parties with beautiful full orchestras playing the most exquisite music. Waltz's so grand I could not stop myself from spinning around as if I were a top. After his death, my grandparents began providing care for us. They were so kind to Mother and me, providing all that we needed. The house we lived in was quite lovely, you know, the one I'm talking about. The Austin stone house that sits on top of Penn Street, looking down to the river."

Mary stopped speaking and looked around, intently trying to focus on where she was. An identifiable tune gently escaped her dry, cracked lips as her eyelids began to relax.

Bettie turned from where she had been looking out the window; one eyebrow raised to a point.

"The Hamilton-Smith house?"

Mary confirmed with a nod.

"My father was a Smith. After he passed, we lived in the carriage house at the bottom of the hill. My grandmother would take me shopping for clothes, hats, and shoes. There was a maid to clean the house and a cook to manage the kitchen. I would've thought this to be a wonderful life for my mother, but she was not content. I was allowed to attend wonderful parties at my grandparents' house until nine in the evening, when I would then be escorted back to the carriage house by one of the butlers. They were required to report back I was safe at home and that my mother was there with me. Mother was not allowed to attend the parties; I never told anyone why."

Mary's breath becoming shallow caused her words to stretch on slowly. Speaking words lost in the past, speaking as if she was reading a script for the first time. Intermittent moments occurred in between the sentences when Waltz Brilliance would bounce across her vocal cords.

"For my tenth birthday, my grandparents threw me the most beautiful birthday party...over one hundred people, most of whom I didn't know. All my favorite foods were served...la da dee la la da...and I was given wonderful gifts. My mother immediately refused them on my behalf—oh, she made an embarrassing scene in front of the guests."

Mary began to doze off, her eyes moving in a rampant back-and-forth motion. Drooling on her chin, she continued to talk faintly, softly.

"There was a great discontent within her, for which I would suffer for years to come...I didn't know anything of what restrictions ...la da dee la la da...were placed on my mother after my father's...death. Mother became very secretive...little patience for the rules imposed on her. Her anger was...overwhelming...la da dee la la da...anyone who crossed her suffered her wrath. I expect if it hadn't been for... me, she would have been cast into the...la da dee la la da...streets without a dime...Mother consistently complained how...they were controlling her to avoid her having... happiness."

Mary's words became labored and monotone as she continued with her tale, her interspersed bits of music now without rhythm or tone. Once again, she stopped, her eyes tightly closed. The opioid, finally in control, forced her into a deep slumber. Bettie moved to her bedside and began to arrange Mary's pillows for comfort, assuming she was out for the count. While Bettie organized the bedding, Mary opened her eyes wide and reached for Bettie's hand. The surprise was two-fold. First was the shock of an almost dead woman reaching out to her, and second was Mary's touch. She had never been affectionate, not to her son, her husband, grandchildren, or anyone. Bettie maintained her composure from the shock and gripped Mary's hand tight, enveloping her fingers. Mary stared at Bettie, her intense, steady gaze again giving in to the medicine. Fading back to slumber, Mary suddenly opened her eyes and looked at Bettie.

"It wasn't until that bastard came along..."

Closing her eyes and relaxing into the pillows, sleep finally was upon her. Bettie unfurled their interwoven digits and gently placed Mary's hand on the bed, tucking the covers neatly around her. Bettie stood for a moment, looking at the body wasting away, staying close should there be another burst of energy or dialogue. A few minutes of silence passed; Bettie reasoned enough time had gone by that it was safe to sit in the handsome brown Naugahyde chair, where she began work on her crochet. It was rare these days she had time to just sit and do her craftwork; the time there was a nice diversion from her daily life, all things considered.

Bettie looked up at Mary often while observing the monitors, confirming heartbeats continued to be counted, and sleep was still in play. She noticed Mary's eyes moving quickly, mumbling incoherently. Every once in a while, a word would slip out, firmly spoken, clear as could be.

Mary shouted out in full voice.

"Stop!"

Bettie immediately looked up to observe the worry showing on Mary's face. She quickly pushed the footstool away from under her feet. Leaving the warm chair, she moved swiftly to the bedside, hoping to provide some physical comfort. She lovingly touched Mary's arm very softly so as to not startle her. Mary yanked her arm away and screamed,

"Don't take my baby! Nooooooooooo!"

Chapter 8

Mary often woke during the night; she was accustomed to hearing the sound of her mother screaming at her father. The outburst from her mother had become so commonplace she didn't bother getting out of bed anymore when hearing it. It was a different sound Mary awoke to this time; it was a guttural moan, a cry emitting from her father. Hearing him call out for her, she ran quickly down the stairs to his study to find him sunken into his favorite chair. The dark-red blood covered his clothes as well as the arms of his chair. The crimson fluid crept across the floor, moving in synch with each remaining pulse. The knife used to slash his wrists lay on the floor beside him, the blade glistening with her father's blood. This moment of terror withdrew her will from her, her body rigid and cold from fright. All she could manage was to stand there, looking at him. Her young mind processed the scene; she felt as if hours passed before the footman appeared. Entering the room through the main double doors, he found Mary and her father alone in the room. His eyes observed the young girl in peril, staring directly at her father's corpse. No one else was in the house but Mary, her mother, her father, and now the footman.

Mary's mother, so uncharacteristically, had given the staff leave for the impending holiday. It was unlike her mother to be so kind and giving, especially during the holidays when there was so much work to be done. The footman had remained on the premises unbeknownst to the matron of the house. He quietly remained out of sight in the stables without comment to anyone about his plan to stay on the estate. With nowhere else he needed or wanted to be, he chose to remain close to his love during the holiday season. Not speaking of this to either of the owners or his work companions allowed him the secrecy required to stay near her.

The large house felt empty and somewhat scary without the servants on site. Mary did not like it when she was home alone with her mother; she preferred the company of her caretaker, Sarah. Sarah treated Mary as if she was her child, providing love and compassion to her, emotions devoid from her mother. There had been occasions when Sarah's children would accompany Sarah to work, helping Cook with meal preparation in the kitchen and assisting with the daily chores. Sarah's offspring, being close to her age, created a curiosity in Mary. She thought it odd they did not dress like her or enjoy afternoon tea. The daily rituals Mary partook in were a part of life; she assumed everyone lived the same as she. Mary was intrigued by Sarah's kids and why they had to perform manual labor at her house. Even though they were completely opposite of her, Mary enjoyed the children being in her home. Engaging with them, she discovered they were content in the kitchen with their mother and the cook; this beguiled Mary. There was a sense of warmth, and often, jeers of laughter would erupt. Behaviors such as these were not allowed in Mary's world, as everything was to be orderly and pristine at all times, no matter the circumstances.

Mary studied ballet and dance with a local teacher who, in her younger days, performed as a principal ballerina in a touring ballet company. From 9 a.m. until 1 p.m. every Monday, Tuesday, and Thursday, lessons were provided for Mary at their home. When Mary wasn't studying dance, and her nanny's kids were at the house, Mary would sneak them up to the second-floor ballroom and dance with them, translating what she had learned from her dance master into movements they would follow. She would have the girls wear hats from her closet and spin around the room, ribbons flowing around and beyond their shoulders, creating a halo of color floating around the room. When the opportunity arose, Mary would steal a hat from her dad's hat rack in his study and hide it in the ballroom. She commanded the boys to wear her father's hats when they entered the hall; she taught them to remove the top hats and bow to the girls when they filed into the ballroom.

Mary called these regular events with her young friends, Cotillions. She didn't understand the concept she had witnessed with her family every spring but loved the spirit of the music being played; the men in tuxedos and the women in ball gowns adorned with beautiful jewelry, enhancing their natural female ornamentation. Mary watched these events with awe, assuming she would spend the rest of her life dancing. Her studies with the former ballerina showed great promise for Mary. She always received a standing ovation when she performed in public at the local theater recitals. It was unclear whether the acclaim was based on her talent or her family's money.

Nevertheless, she adored the stage and hoped to show the world her gifted toe shoes someday. Before being dismissed for bed by her father at the spring dances, he always requested Waltz Brilliance be played by the orchestra. This was his and Mary's special dance. Anyone attending the parties at the estate more than once knew the unique nature between these two. With the first downbeat from the conductor, the dance floor would clear, allowing her and her father to have their special dance alone. The guests left to admire the lovely couple spinning around the room. This was her special time with her father, an unbreakable bond created that would never leave her. Oh, how she loved to dance, especially with her father.

But that would be no more.

The footman stood there looking at her father with an evil smile. Mary observed the smirk and became nervous as she did not like this man; she sensed him to be cruel. Sarah made sure Mary was never alone when this man was nearby for reasons that only Sarah knew.

As Mary witnessed the last trickle of blood leave her dad's wrist, her mother entered the room, pacing slowly like a Jaguar, calm and poised, ready to strike. Advancing as if she had won a prize for slaying her prey. Looking at Mary, she ordered her daughter to leave the room. On her mother's command, Mary quickly ran into the hallway, freezing at the bottom of the stairs; she didn't know what to do or where to go. Standing there in shock, she heard her mother say,

"Well, now that's done!"

This was to be one of the many scars inflicted on Mary by her mother. In her frozen state on the landing, she heard her mother continue with directions.

"The police need to be summoned, and you need not be here. Why didn't you leave with the rest of the staff?"

Mary's mother spoke to the footman with care in her voice. Mary could not recall having ever heard these inflections from her before.

"Why did you come into the house? You were not supposed to be here. This will bring up questions which are unnecessary. This was not the plan we had agreed to."

"I heard screaming, didn't know if something had gone wrong. Thought it might be you."

The footman replied with an overly concerned tone.

Her mother paused while surveying the room.

"Don't worry about Mary; I will manage who she speaks to. I will tell her if she doesn't do what I say, I will send Sarah and her children away."

Mary's mother, speaking with the air of superiority in her voice that Mary was accustomed to, once again surveyed the room.

Mary began to tiptoe up the stairs to her room, numb from all she had just witnessed. Reaching the top of the stairs, she peered down through the banister railing to see her mother opening the front door, the footman close at heel. Her mother stood holding the door open for the footman to leave. When he reached the door, he leaned in and kissed her ever so softly on the lips. Her mother didn't recoil, didn't react, only received it. Walking through the door, his lover reminded him their entanglement must remain a secret until an appropriate amount of time passed. She could not risk anyone suspecting anything; she must be sure the estate was hers without question.

One more emotional scar for Mary; it was all about the money.

Her mother closed the door, fully aware Mary had observed this interaction. Quietly she turned the lock on the door before rotating her head up to look at Mary.

"You will never speak of what you have seen or heard this evening. Should you choose not to obey me, I will send Sarah and her children back to where they came from. You wouldn't want to see Sarah and her family suffer, would you? Now go to your room and remain there until I come for you."

Mary ran to her room, locking the door behind her. She knew this didn't make sense, for her mother had keys to the room, but it somehow helped her feel safe. She lay in her bed, reeling from the events she had observed. Sleep evaded her for fear her mother would do something evil to her. Trying her best to stay awake, the moment arrived when she could no longer resist, and she was asleep.

As the sun began shining small slivers of light into her room, she awoke, quickly looking around the room. For a moment, she thought this must have all been a bad dream. Immediately she felt better, the worry subsiding in her. A few moments had passed when Sarah entered the room; this confirmed it had all been a nightmare. Sarah did not have keys to unlock the door, suggesting Mary had never locked it. She was beginning to recover, happy the horrible visions had been only that.

Sarah, at the edge of her bed, presented the warm, loving smile Mary joyously received from her every day. Pulling Mary into her arms, holding her tight against her bosom. Mary loved being in Sarah's arms; it was safe and warm. She had never been held by her mother, as best she could recall.

Unbeknownst to Mary, a child had been a requirement of the marriage between her mother and father, Mr. Tristen

Smith. If an heir was provided to perpetuate the Smith family name, the wife was free to live her life; however she wanted. A daughter being born suggested the family name would not continue on, assuming she would marry someday. This did not alter the love Tristen Smith felt for his daughter; Mary was treated as if she were a queen, the best of everything for her; her mother never consulted. He demanded Sarah take care of Mary as if she were her own; in return, he paid Sarah beyond the standard rate for any nanny. Tristen didn't like his wife, nor did he trust her. She had failed at providing him with a son, and there was no need for her anymore.

When notice was given to the staff that they would have the holiday with their families, Sarah requested Mary celebrate the festivities at her home with her children.

Mary's mother denied the request.

"You take care of your family, and I will take care of mine."

She would have none of Sarah's inappropriate offer; she needed Mary at home this holiday.

Sarah continued holding Mary, carrying her into the bath where the tub was filled with warm water, waiting for little Mary. Sarah kneeled, standing Mary on the floor.

"I know this isn't when we normally bathe, but we have to wash this blood off of you, baby."

It was then Mary realized the nightmare was indeed reality. Mary looked down to see her feet stained with her father's blood that had pooled on the floor.

The police were summoned the next morning while Sarah was retrieved from her home, arriving just before the officers did. Mrs. Smith waited just long enough before making the calls to ensure her playmate was quietly away but soon enough for her story to be plausible. The police performed their investigation and deemed the incident a suicide, matching the premise laid out by the grieving wife. No suicide note was found, but due to where the cuts were, no other probable cause was sought. The knife on the floor beside him, the cuts on each wrist, precision crisscrosses, no signs of struggle or any bruising apparent, all signs pointed to the same conclusion. What else could it be? The staff were all gone, the daughter asleep. It all made perfect sense.

Only to follow protocol, the police requested they be allowed to question Mary. No matter how they pleaded with her, she would not speak to them. The head detective arrived at the conclusion Mary was in shock, and therefore they were wasting everyone's time. While the adults talked about the tragedy, Mary thought of the blood on her feet. Surely the bloody footprints on the carpets in the stairwell leading to her room were a clue. While the police discussed the matter with Mrs. Smith, Mary leaped from her chair running to the door, startling everyone in the room. She looked at the carpet and up the stairs to only discover they were clean and free of any debris. Her mother must have cleaned them while she slept. Sarah was the only one who knew the truth besides little Mary; the police never questioned the dark-skinned servant.

The incident was declared self-inflicted, and the case was closed.

Being quite anxious about the estate being settled, the next three months were painfully slow for Mrs. Smith. Time passed unhurriedly for Mary's mother with the footman lying in wait. During this time, all the staff re-mained in service and on-site, carrying on their daily du-ties as if nothing had changed. With the exception being her father being gone, little had changed in their daily routine.

The Widow Smith was confident her in-laws would do whatever they could to keep her from getting anything. Part of her agreement with Tristen was to provide an heir; also included was a provision that should she ever be found out to be unfaithful to the Smith name, she would be cast out without a cent. In return for maintaining propriety, her husband's will stated she would receive all that was due to her. The intent was to ensure Mary had the best of things and be appropriately taken care of as long as financial subsidies were maintained.

The status quo was maintained until one evening when Sarah was leaving Mary's room and saw the footman leaving the master bedroom. The rumors began to spread, not only in the household but around the community. The elder, Mr. Smith, heard tell of the scandal from his barber and immediately summoned Mary's mother to his office. She dismissed the rumors, denying knowing the footman by name. She must have been quite convincing as Mary's grandfather released her without question. Upon returning home that day, Mrs. Smith relieved the staff of their duties, everyone except the footman and Sarah. Mary was not aware of the conversation between her mother and Sarah after the help was terminated, only that Sarah was now very quiet and no longer affectionate with her.

Finally, the day her mother had been waiting for arrived, the last will and testament of Tristen Smith was to be read. The lawyer's office filled with family members and former and current staff. Mary was made to wait in the outer office during the lengthy process. The reading of Tristen's will revealed college funds for each of the staff's children and pension funds for all who had served his family while he was alive. In addition to the college funds for Sarah's children, she would receive a sum large enough that she would never have to work again if she so chose. Tristen made a note of all her dutiful work, acknowledging his appreciation for being a proper female figure for Mary. A sizable amount of money was bequeathed to the new performance hall, which would later bear his name. With little patience on Mrs. Smith's part, the reading finally turned to her. It was at this point the attorney dismissed everyone from the room to gain their respective signatures and finalize the details with his legal secretary. With their exit, he called Mary into the office before continuing with her mother's misfortune. Mary's mother openly spoke of her disapproval of Mary being present. The lawyer looked up from his papers before addressing the room.

"The rest of the will concerns her and how you are to behave in regards to her. She has a right to hear her father's last wishes."

The lawyer spelled out the terms noting the estate would be returned to the parents of Tristen Smith. In return, Mary would be provided a proper home near the elder Smiths. Mary's mother was to live with her and raise her appropriately. She was to prepare Mary for a future where she would be endowed with her portion of the estate at the age of twenty-one. Mary's mother was furious at this turn of events. How could Tristen have changed things and not followed through with his promise? He did as she asked; she got what he felt she deserved. She cursed at the grandparents, spewing vile threats, including her intent to contest the will. Mary's grandmother, who spoke with kindness to everyone she encountered, rose to her feet and escorted Mary to the outer waiting room. She asked Mary to quietly remain in the outer office while she spoke to Mary's mother in private. Closing the lawyer's office door, the elder Mrs. Smith spoke with firmness and disdain.

"We will not press charges against you for the murder of our son if you abide by his will. You should have used more discretion when sleeping with your servant, who liked to brag about your sexual escapades at the local pub. Did you not think he could be bought if the price was right? Did you not think Sarah would confide in me about the bloodstains she removed from Mary's feet and bed linens? We will abide by my son's will for Mary's sake, no reason more."

Returning to her seat, meeting Mary's mother's gaze straight on, she asked the attorney to continue. Mary and her mother were to move immediately, as their house had been sold. The elder, Mr. Smith, opted to sell the estate to fund Tristen's bequest and make investments in Mary's best interest.

Leaving the lawyer's office, Mary was pulled up from her chair and led out of the office by her mother. Forcefully dragged by one arm down the stairs and out of the building. They rode back to the home, no longer theirs, in complete silence. Moving slowly around the circular drive, the marble steps closed in. Mary jumped from the carriage, running up the stone staircase and through the ornate ten-foot-high, double-hung, walnut doors for the last time. Passing through the open door, Mary felt her mother grab her by the shoulder, quickly spinning her around to face her mother.

"You will pay me back for all you have taken from me!"

The next five years in the carriage house were good for Mary and passed quickly. Her grandparents took care of her, leaving her to never want for anything other than her mother's love. What she received instead was disdain from the woman who bore her. She was now blossoming into a woman, with subtle changes happening in her. Her mother taunted her for turning into a woman prematurely.

"It's not normal, but then again, you are just like your father—abnormal!"

Mary's mother didn't explain to her what was happening to her body. After being called abnormal, she refused to ask any questions about herself to her grandmother, or the housekeeper; if she was going to be a freak, she didn't want anyone to know.

Later that year, her grandmother took ill, dying unexpectedly. Mary, sad to see her pass, never shed a tear; she had blocked that emotional floodgate upon her father's death. All the cruel things she endured forced her to lock away her emotions; it was the only way to maintain her ability to be in society. She was never happy or sad; she just existed. A few months after her grandmother died, her grandfather suffered a massive stroke leaving him incapacitated. His future would consist of his day-to-day life managed in a convalescence home. When the elder Mr. Smith was settled into his new home, Mary's mother decided it was time to contest the will and get what she thought was due to her. The judge, reviewing her contestation of the will, exercised his ruling power stating too much time had passed; the courts denied her plea. With this last outrage cast upon her, she began taking every bit of anger out on Mary. She didn't physically hit her; the damage done with words was far worse than any physical punishment. They were moved out of the carriage house into town, into a small apartment owned by the Smith family, used for visitors who weren't suitable to stay at the estate. Mary's grandfather deeded the residence to Mary shortly after his wife passed. His intent was to provide her with a home, no matter what the future might deliver. This turned out to be a sage move on his part, as within a year of his stroke, the Smith Family was bankrupt. The men who remained in charge of the family businesses paid themselves handsomely; huge salaries and bonuses bled the company dry. While reading the paper, Mary learned of her grandfather's death; Mr. Smith died the same day the bankruptcy was declared.

Mary and her mother moved into a second-floor apartment in the building Mary owned. Her mother had no knowledge of her daughter's name on the deed. With the footman betrayal behind them, Mary's mother began dating a new gentleman. The man was obnoxious and usually drunk, constantly cursing at everything. He was the complete opposite of the men Mary had grown up around. He walked around the house without clothes, showing his body to Mary in all states of arousal. Mary thought him to be vulgar and disgusting. Her mother began drinking excessively to keep up with her new friend. Mary repeatedly would awaken in the mornings to find them passed out in the parlor in various stages of undress. To avoid the drunken duo, Mary often left the apartment via the fire escape.

Venturing off to the library where she could read books and magazines without fear of being found or harassed. On her way to the library to read magazines and newspapers, Mary would pass a dance studio for young women; she often stood there for hours watching the young girls in positions 1, 2, 3, and so on. On occasion, she would pirouette along with them, forgetting she was on the street in front of the building. Admiring her form and beauty, the instructor exited the studio one afternoon and invited Mary to join. Without money or means for proper dance attire, Mary politely declined the invitation.

Along with her forever love of dance, a deep passion erupted within Mary, reading fashion magazines. She read every article she found on couture in New York and

Paris; this passion led her to spend time near the department stores downtown. Observing how the ladies dressed, walked, and spoke, she fell madly in love with it all. The hair, the makeup, the allure they presented. She also noticed how the prettier a woman was, the better she was treated.

Unbeknownst to her mother, she began to earn a little money, making deliveries for one of the department stores nearby. Mary saved the money she earned, so she might purchase some colorful yarn and a pattern book with knitting needles included. Whenever her mother was passed out from her drinking, Mary would hide in her room, where she would produce little sweaters or hats with the yarn she obtained. All her work was hidden away from her mother, fearing her mother would take them from her. When Mary had finished an item to her satisfaction, she would find a local store and attempt to sell them to the proprietor. Each penny made put away, hidden from her mother and the horrible man living with them, saving up until she could afford to buy more supplies.

Coming home one late evening, assuming her housemates would be drunk and rowdy, Mary headed for her apartment via the fire escape. She often used the alternate apartment entrance to come and go; the window in her room allowed her to avoid her family as much as possible. She chose to not deal with her mother or her companion unless forced to. Generally speaking, when it came to her, out of sight meant out of mind for her parents.

Due to the slight chill in the air, Mary hurriedly ascended the ladder leading to her room. When she reached the landing outside her window, there he was, sitting in the corner, waiting for her. Attempting to return back down the ladder, he grabbed her by the arm, pulling her tightly into him. He looked down at her, his stare cold and dark. His eyes penetrated through her skin, peering deep into her soul. A chill from fear went right through her. She tried pulling away from him but feared if she pulled too hard, she might lose footing on the landing and fall back down the metal stairs. Her eyes darted to the window, which was still ajar; she leaped through the opening, hoping to close it before he could enter. Once again, he was too fast, seemingly flying through the window simultaneously with her. He wrapped his arms around her, pulling her close against his bulging trousers. Numerous times she had observed him naked, sporting an erection. Now his member was firm and pressed against her body. The more she twisted to get away from his erection, the more aroused he became. Her stomach was turning, feeling him so close to her; his aroused state scared her.

"You know what that whore of a mother you have, has done?"

He screamed at her while violently grabbing at her. With one hand, he shoved her hard against the wall, his hand resting on her neck.

She began to tremble from head to toe, the room feeling like it was twenty degrees. Her mind racing, not knowing how to respond, she shivered in his shadow.

"She got me all hard and anxious, then told me I would have to wait until she was ready for me. Poured herself a drink and passed out in bed. I have been sitting here, waiting for you."

Pointing to the bulge in his pants,

"You are going to take care of this!"

Mary attempted to scream out for help; it was a futile effort as he had her pinned so tightly against the wall she could barely inhale, much less scream. His free hand ran across her breast with a single finger landing on her lips as he unfurled his fist. His index finger slowly moved down her neck, landing between her breasts, ripping her dress open as his finger slid down her middle past her navel, slipping into her panties. With one swift move, he ripped them off her, tossing them across the room. Again she tried to scream but was unable to make a sound. Multiple fingers now massaged her newly formed pubic hair before forcing them deep inside her. The pain she encountered was unlike any she had ever known; so intense she felt as if she might pass out. Withdrawing the bloodied fingers from inside her, he dragged her onto the bed, one hand holding her by the throat. His pants falling to the floor, he mounted her. Closing her eyes to avoid seeing his angry face, she cried out silently while he forced himself inside her. Keeping her pinned down with one arm, he used the other as a fulcrum to increase the strength of his thrust. Mary attempted to move her legs tightly together in hopes of reducing the depth of his penetration. He forced his knee between her thighs, pushing them back apart. The more she resisted, the more excited and forceful he became. He moaned out loud with pleasure from her virgin body, cursing at her while pleasuring himself.

Finishing his deed, he pulled out of her in one swift movement. Stumbling backward towards the bedroom door, he grabbed his pants and exited the room. She lay there in silence, attempting to scream out, but no sounds came. Tears rolled down her cheeks as she looked up to find her mother's shadow in the doorway. Her mother slunk into the room, cocktail in hand, ice clinking with each step she took. Making her way to where Mary lay, she leaned in close and said,

"This is how you will pay me back for what you fucking took from me!"

Standing next to the bed where her young daughter had just been defiled, she merely stared at her. Finally turning to walk out of the room, she giggled as she called out to ask if he had fun.

Two days later, Mary, her mother, and he were packed up and on their way to Oklahoma City. Her mother, marrying the rapist, decided there was no need to stay in that godforsaken western town any longer. Being forced into the car's jump seat, Mary saw her mother settling into the front seat. The pedophile crawled into the driver's seat, turned to Mary's mother, and gave her a kiss. Her mother, glancing over her shoulder at Mary, smiled and said,

"Say hello to your new daddy."

As they drove the county roads north to a new life, Mary was filled with dread and terror. Mary was soon to be fifteen with nothing to look forward to.

The weeks that followed were mindless for Mary; she did whatever she was told to do without question. Every night, Daddy would come into her room and service himself with her flesh. She learned to distance herself by thinking of places she read about in fashion books. Someday she would be able to say no to this, she hoped.

Three months had passed in the new city; Mary was doing her best to find her way around, making several attempts to sell her knitted baby clothes to the stores, but no one showed interest. Returning to Simpson's Department Store, hoping to wear the owner down, she struck up a conversation with the owner's wife. The lovely cherub-faced woman didn't realize Mary's purpose was to sell the baby clothes to her husband; she thought her to be a new customer. During the conversation, Mary unbuttoned her coat. While removing her scarf, Mary felt Mrs. Simpson's hand on her stomach.

Looking Mary straight in the eye, she patted her belly.

"Are you wanting a boy or a girl?"

"I don't understand what you are asking me, Ma'am."

The store owner's wife was caught off guard by Mary's response. Mrs. Simpson went on,

"Oh dear, my apologies. You look to me to be pregnant."

The next thing Mary remembered was waking up on the couch in the owner's storeroom. Coming to, she opened her eyes to find a young man standing over her.

Mary inquired,

"Who are you? Where am I?"

"You passed out in the store. You're in Simpson's Department Store!"

The young man called out from the storeroom.

"Hey, Mr. Simpson, she's awake!"

A few seconds passed before a portly gentleman in a bland suit with a matching waistcoat pushed through the swinging doors.

"You gave us quite a fright, little lady."

The store owner stopped just shy of the sofa Mary rested on.

"Are you okay?"

Mary gathered her thoughts and shook her head yes.

Mrs. Simpson touched Thadeus on the shoulder.

"Thadeus, walk her home and make sure you tell her parents she passed out in the store."

Mr. Simpson turned his gaze to Mary, assessing her.

"Young lady, are you in a delicate situation? Do you have a husband? Does your family know?"

Mary sat quietly, trying to form her words.

"I don't believe I am in a family way, sir. I believe it just might be a cold."

"What's your family name?"

Mr. Simpson knew something was off, and he didn't want any nonsense in his store.

"My last name is Smith, but my mother has remarried and has a different last name. I don't recall what it is."

Mary was very sheepish, her head spinning from the suggestion she might be pregnant.

Mr. Simpson turned away from her and motioned his clerk to come out front with him. In a few minutes, Thadeus returned and offered his hand to help her up off the couch.

"Let me walk you home; I promise I won't say a word to anyone about what happened here today or Mr. Simpson's suspicions about you. I will just make sure you get home safe."

For some unknown reason to her, Mary believed him and trusted him to do what he said. As they walked through the streets of the City, huddling close in the cold, he shared his philosophy with Mary.

"I believe what you do should be your own business. I don't want anybody knowing my business, so why should I be worried about your business."

This was reassuring to Mary. She felt like she could depend on him to stay quiet. After leaving her in front of her building, Thadeus turned to walk back to the store. Rounding the corner on the backside of the apartment building, out of nowhere, a drunken man grabbed him by the shoulder, screaming at him,

"You stay away from my stepdaughter. She belongs to me! If you touch her, I will cut your balls off! Who the hell are you?"

Reacting in fear and surprise, Thadeus began to babble.

"I work for Mr. Simpson—he told me to walk her home and make sure she was safe! You see, she fainted in the store. She said it was a cold or something, but Mrs. Simpson seemed to think it was otherwise."

Thadeus spoke without thinking, forgetting his commitment to Mary to maintain silence.

Mary's stepfather let Thadeus loose, stumbling backward a bit from what the boy had said. Released from the man's grip, Thadeus was off and running as fast and far away as he could.

Even in his drunken state, he knew what this meant. He stumbled back to the apartment and told Mary's mom what had happened. She leaned back in her velveteen chair and took a long slow drink followed by a deep inhalation of her cigarette. Pondering her options before speaking.

"We will just have to fix this."

Mary awoke in the hospital, knowing something was horribly wrong. Through the weariness in her head, she felt unbearable pain in her stomach. She reached down and touched the incision closed by the stitches across her abdomen. She was swollen and weak. She cried out for help with no response. A few minutes later, a doctor entered the room, asking her to lie still. Injecting her arm with sedatives, he informed her she would remain in that bed for a week.

"What have you done to me?"

"I did what your mother asked me to do. I agree with your mother on this; if you insist on going around being a loose woman, this will prevent you from ever getting pregnant again. We don't need women like you bringing children into this world."

Looking her in the eyes, he shook his head in disgust before leaving the room. She heard him call out to her mother, announcing Mary was coming around but would soon return to sleep. Mary's mother entered the room wearing the same evil grin Mary saw the day her dad died. Her mother stopped at the foot of the bed and stared at her daughter like an evil queen surveying her subjects. Her air of superiority danced around the room. Waltzing up to the head of the bed, she looked at her daughter and grinned her evil smile.

"Now, your new daddy can do his business whenever he wants, and we won't have to worry about any more babies coming along. You be a good girl and get some rest. We will come back to take you home next week after you have healed."

After her mother left, Mary began to cry over the loss of her child. The sedation, taking effect, lessened the tears. It was then that a familiar face came into view. In her semi-conscious state, Mary couldn't comprehend why she knew the nurse tending to her wounds. Quietly and quickly, the woman dressed all in white applied iodine to the freshly cut skin before she replaced the bandages. Observing the extent of the surgery performed on Mary, in complete disagreement with what had been done to this young girl, she began to comfort her.

"You poor dear, this is all so wrong; what makes them think this is OK? What a terrible thing they have done to you! Have faith, my dear, and you will get out of this mess alive."

Mrs. Simpson left a gentle kiss on Mary's forehead before turning to go.

Five days later, Mary disappeared from the hospital, wearing a borrowed nurse's uniform.

She would never see her mother again.

Chapter 9

After much soul-searching and deliberation, Sheriff Turner decided he would leave Carter County. Should he stay, every scenario played out in his head pointed to the same outcome; he would remain alone. It was time for him to start over, to find a new home where he believed he could be the man he really was.

He never knew what happened to Aaron but often thought about him. His life had become lonely, with nothing but his work to consume his time. It had been four months since his beautiful, loving wife, Ida, had passed away. He knew he would never find another wife who understood his need for male companionship or who would enjoy a relationship like the one they had with Aaron. Living a solitary existence was a choice for him, as he would never love another man like Aaron. For him, it was a love that could not be emulated or replaced. His marriage to Ida had initially been out of convenience, a means to an end, a union not built on sexual compatibility. This, in turn, led to a relationship built out of great intimacy, something far more meaningful than just a physical partnership. He missed her so much; she had become the one true confidant he had in life. He longed to have her back every waking moment. His wife maintained his secret about Aaron, often dispelling rumors about her husband. No one could ever know about their relationship with Aaron, or her husband would have been lynched for sure. The two loves of his life were now gone; this job, this county, this sad life, was all he had.

That night, alone at home, sitting in his wife's rocking chair, he examined the last piece of needlework she had been working on. He recalled their trip to Honey Creek, where she had been stitching this hoop fitted with white linen; the morning she sat with Beatrice during her first monthly visitor. He had never paid much attention to the contents of her needlepoint; he thought it to be silly statements of well-being. Holding the hoop stitched in gold thread on white cloth in his hand, he read, "Love will lead the way." He recognized it as a message from his late wife. This moment of angelic intervention set a series of events in action, altering lives forever.

After seeing the needlepoint by his wife's chair, he knew it was right to go; there was no longer a reason to stay. Thinking back on all he had missed out on by not being true to himself, he acknowledged he had grieved his losses long enough. His wife's illness had physically and emotionally drained him; it was his turn to recoup. The end of her life came as a blessing, an end releasing him from a constant state of worry and caregiving. In the time since Ida had passed, he dealt with this nagging emotion, telling him he was better suited to live a life elsewhere. Somewhere far away from this place, somewhere every man could be himself without living in fear of openly loving whomever he chose.

Convincing himself leaving Carter County was an appropriate course of action, he decided he should visit his wife's grave to say goodbye and seek forgiveness for leaving her. Driving to the cemetery, he felt a spirit rumbling inside him, a nervousness stirring he had not felt before. Driving through the wrought iron gates, he took the first road, making a right turn on the grey pea gravel. The car tires crunching the stone as he drove slowly along the rock wall encircling the cemetery. He decided he would park on the outer edge of the graveyard near the wall, far removed from the headstones sitting on top of their respective corpses. He walked across the untouched ground, his pace slow and exact as he made his way to the plot where he left his wife for the last time. A strong sense of peace had come upon him while making his way across the graveyard. He gingerly sat down atop her grave, letting his mind roam; he found a meditative state enhanced by the calm that had overtaken him. Sitting there, the time quickly passed, and before he was aware, the sun had begun to fall behind the tree break on the western side of the cemetery. He was lost in a sense of warmth and compassion, as if his late wife had wrapped her arms around him, lovingly whispering to him, coercing him to move on with his life.

His mind's ear heard her,

"David, go and find happiness, my love—he is out there waiting for you."

Returning back to cognition from his meditative state, he noticed how beautiful the sunset was; the warm orange and gold colors were soft and serene. With the sun setting, he began to feel the chill of the night air creeping upon him, returning him to the present world he had mentally stepped out of. Pulling himself up to a kneeling position in front of her headstone, he leaned forward and placed an attentive kiss on her photo embedded in the stone. Rising to walk away from the grave very slowly, he embraced every sound and sight he encountered, tucking them away in his heart so he would never lose them. He could still hear her voice guiding him, repeating what she had said, he is out there waiting for you. Retracing his meditative journey, the suggestion she made he leave became real to him. He pondered what she meant; what an oddity to use the term "He." Was he just hoping against hope? Was Ida foreshadowing his future? Could a love for him be somewhere waiting for him?

He stopped before reaching the small gravel road where he had left his cruiser; he turned and looked back at the headstone and blew it a kiss. He was fully confident in moving forward, knowing any future was better than what he could have here. He crossed the road and opened the car door; climbing into the front seat, he gently pulled the door closed. He peered once more at her headstone, seeing a beautiful Monarch butterfly landing just above her name. Her wings moved slowly, suggesting time had slowed for the moment. He knew this was a sign. Following the metaphysical conversation he had just encountered, this was his beloved wife waving farewell.

Driving away, past the iron cemetery gates, David decided he must also take Beatrice away from all of this. He began working out his plan to leave without suspicion, intently reviewing it numerous times in his head. What was needed? Who might ask questions? What to do if discovered?

Once he felt he had the plan configured to the nth degree, he began the process by quietly purchasing a new car. As he always drove the county car, there had never been a need for one of his own. He knew he must obtain the automobile out of state, far away from anyone who might know him or his position in law enforcement. He began this adventure dressed in ratty clothes walking down the Denton highway, thumbing his way to Texas. Reaching a small gas station just past the edge of town, he offered a man who had just settled his bill with the attendant a few bucks to drive him to his destination. He supplied the man with a friendly smile along with the pretense he was going to Texas to look for work and a place to build a life. The small-framed man whose car carried Illinois plates was traveling through Oklahoma on his way to Dallas. He decided the handsome hobo would be pleasant company. In just a short amount of time, they arrived in Sherman, Texas. David thanked the man with two one-dollar bills and a firm handshake; grabbing his rolled-up belongings lying on the seat next to him, he exited the car and waved goodbye to the small stranger. Once the Illinois tags were out of sight, he headed off to change clothes in a nearby gas station restroom. It was important he shift his appearance from bum to businessman. He knew a man dressed like a bum would receive unwanted attention in a car dealership, just the same as a man in a suit bumming a ride across state lines would beg questions. David exited the facilities dressed in a modest grey tweed suit with a white shirt and dark tie. His shoes were the only thing he thought might give him away; he dusted them as best as possible with the rags he had been wearing. With the shoes polished, he disposed of the worn-out jeans and red flannel shirt, tossing them into a nearby trashcan. Returning to the street, David began to make his way to the car dealership to make his purchase. Being dressed in a shirt and tie, he didn't have to walk far before a local businessman offered him a ride into town. He explained to his new traveling companion his car had broken down, and he was attempting to arrive at the dealership before they closed. The elderly gentleman acknowledged the challenges with these new contraptions, confirming how much he missed his horse and buggy. While lamenting about the modern changes occurring around him daily, he said he was happy to assist the young man. The kind older gentleman dropped David off at the front step of the automobile salesroom; moving merrily on his way, he merged back into traffic towards his original destination. Walking through the front doors of the dealership, David was quickly greeted by an eager salesman, happy to share his automobile expertise with his new best friend. After selecting the basic black Oldsmobile sedan, he handed cash to the finance manager, signed the paperwork, and drove north to the Sheriff's office in Ardmore. He discreetly parked the car on the street behind the station. Should anyone question it being there, he would report it having been left there by Pretty Man. That would most assuredly cease any and all questions. Even if someone saw him park it, the suit and hat he wore would throw them off. No one would expect the Sheriff to be out of uniform and dressed in stylish clothes. People around the county never saw him in anything except his uniform or work clothes. Besides, a connection to Pretty Man generally encouraged people to turn a blind eye.

It was two days before his planned escape, the date chosen perfectly timed to coincide with his scheduled visit to check on Leroy. Edgar knew, once every ninety days, Sheriff Turner would be out to see if Leroy was still alive or if perhaps he had run away. This wasn't a requirement by the prison system; David just used it as an excuse to visit Beatrice without any questions. With no other known felons living in Carter County, he could easily make this fabrication work.

Waking up early the next morning, Sheriff Turner drove the county car on the ungraded road towards the run-down shack; turning into the farm's entrance, he saw Beatrice in the garden working. She looked up from where she was tilling the dirt around her vegetables, realizing it was he; Beatrice smiled while managing herself up off the ground where she knelt. When she finally erected herself, she began slowly walking towards him. As she made her way towards him, he spotted the roundness in her belly. Immediately he realized he was too late to get her away without harm. Regretting he had not acted sooner, the Sheriff was saddened by the situation. He exited the cruiser; remaining near the door-mounted spotlight, he observed how tired she appeared. She stopped just a few feet from Sheriff Turner; just as she began to converse with David, Edgar made his presence known. Leaving the shack's front door, he kicked the screen door, opening it a full 180 degrees, and slamming it into the side of the house before it swung back into him. This was a blessing in disguise; had they spoken about anything of importance, it would have probably been overheard.

Edgar shouted to the Sheriff,

"You here to check on Leroy?"

The Sheriff looked up to where Edgar stood before responding.

"Where is he? Has he run off yet?"

Edgar turned around, shouting out with his cranky bellowing voice that could not be missed.

"Leroy—get your butt up here for the Sheriff!"

No response was heard; he boomed again,

"Leroy!"

Edgar repeated himself a third time, still nothing but silence.

"Goddamnit!"

Assessing the Sheriff's stance, he altered his approach to the situation.

"I'll go see if he's in the outhouse."

Edgar suspected Leroy was down at the still drinking; this irritated him more than usual. Money was being wasted, as well as Leroy knew this was the day of the Sheriff's visit. Not wanting the Sheriff to see where he was headed, Edgar turned back into the house, walking through it to go out the back door. The Sheriff knew if he was going to save her from this awful entrapment, he must act quickly. Beatrice was most likely unknown to anyone, as she had never been allowed to leave the homestead. Besides the information she would have learned reading the books Ida had provided over the years, Beatrice would know little of the world beyond the boundaries of the land she grew up on. Before speaking to Beatrice, the Sheriff thought about how taking her away posed many risks to both of them.

"Do you want to leave this place?"

He asked very softly so as to not be overheard.

Beatrice paused before answering simply,

"Yep—please."

David quickly and cautiously looked around before giving directions.

"Your dad will make his usual run to the City tomorrow night. After he leaves, go to the road and wait for me. I will pick you up in a car. Be clear on this—I will not be in the Sheriff's car. Understand?"

Beatrice shook her head up and down, indicating yes. She stopped and looked up at him.

"What about Leroy? He gets on top of me whenever Dad goes away."

David had not thought about Leroy; he assumed Leroy would be with Edgar. Unknowingly, Beatrice answered the question on David's mind about who the baby's father was. Despite his occupation, he did his best to not live in judgment of others. Living with the freedom of love he experienced with his late wife, David did not believe in placing his moral compass on others, but for some reason, he was disgusted by this. He heard someone in the house stumbling across the wooden floors. David wrapped things up quickly before anyone appeared.

"Just be where I told you. I will take care of the rest."

Leroy stumbled out the front door, shouting from the porch.

"I'm here, you fucker—will you be happy for another ninety days!"

Sheriff Turner knew he needed to make his presence understood. He walked around the front of the car, passing Beatrice without looking at her. He stood tall and walked with precision creating an imposing strong demeanor, visually reminding Leroy he ultimately had control. His pace was slow but deliberate. Approaching the steps, he stared Leroy down.

"Would you like to spend a few days in the jailhouse? Speak to me again like that, and that's where you will end up!"

Leroy backed down, knowing this wasn't a fight he could win, especially in his drunken state.

Sheriff Turner continued to stare him in the eyes while he waited for an affirmation from Leroy. Finally receiving it, he slowly turned around, heading back to the car. Noticing Beatrice had taken the opportunity to leave the scene, David sat down in his cruiser, convinced the plan would work. As he drove away, he hoped she understood his directions and would be there when he returned the next evening.

Beatrice was overwhelmed by the possibility she could leave and start a new life. She realized she had no way of knowing what the world could be like, but felt anything beyond this life would be an improvement. She had been provided mercy so many times; the young girl alongside her brothers who took the time to bury her mother with her babies, the Sheriff, and his wife, and the shadow in the woods watching over her. Thinking about all these times, she took leave of her chores and walked to the graves of her mother and siblings. As she walked through the woods, she thought back through the years, realizing how little had changed. The occasional appearance by her angel, along with the child growing inside her, was all that appeared to alter. She had come to believe there were forces beyond her understanding operating around her; she accepted them for the good she believed they intended. She arrived at the stone marking her mother's grave; crawling to the ground to sit, she began to cry. Not being sure if she should leave this place, sadness overcame her. But a voice deep inside her said she should go if she didn't want her unborn child to suffer. If she had a girl, the same terrible acts of violence would be placed upon her; if she had a son, he would be taught to be like Edgar or Leroy. Now with an option to get away, she became determined to do whatever it took to provide her child a fighting chance. As she tired from the emotional turmoil, she stretched out in the grass to rest before her journey. She recalled how this place had always been her refuge in times of trouble; she would most surely miss it. Stretching out her arms and legs, extending them to be as long as she could, she relaxed, letting the morning sun warm her; soon, she fell into a deep rest much needed for her days ahead. Forcing the worries of survival out of her head, she knew her prayers for salvation had been heard.

Coming out of the deep sleep, she realized she was late preparing supper for her father and brother. Even though she was pregnant, he would not relent from striking her if she failed at fulfilling her imposed duties. She pushed herself up from the dirt bed and returned as quickly as she could to the shack. Salvation had already begun, as neither Leroy nor her dad was there. She immediately lit the stove, working as fast as she could. Finally, the cooktop reached the temperature necessary to melt the lard in the cast iron skillet sitting atop it. The okra enveloped in cornmeal was ready for the frying pan; the tomatoes were cut and resting in flour, awaiting their turn in the scalding liquid. Turning to the stove, she gently sifted the okra into the skillet when out of nowhere, she heard a loud roar permeate the house. She had never heard such an invasive noise; so intense in its presence, soot from the heat pipe floated into the air. She momentarily stopped placing the food into the hot oil, wondering where the thunder could have come from. She had just come from outdoors; there wasn't a cloud in the sky. Unexpectedly a second round of noise encroached on the house, louder than the first. Shaking the utensils on the table, flour on the sliced tomatoes convulsing on their host. Quickly she approached the door to determine where this ruckus was coming from; pushing open the back screen door, she saw the orange ball of flames fly upwards into the air heading into the sky. If she had care or concern for her father or brother, it might have consumed her, but there was none. She caught a glimpse of her father out of her periphery, running towards the orange ball, appearing to grow in size. She turned to see where he had come from and noticed the truck partially loaded for tomorrow's run, several jugs on the ground outside their crates scattered as if they had been thrown. Edgar ran past her while repeatedly screaming out for Leroy. Calling time after time for her brother, the call more frantic with each step. Observing all the commotion from the back porch, she noticed the smell of smoke in the house. Her immediate thought was the massive ball of fire had landed on the roof; it was merely the skillet full of okra catching fire. For a brief moment before applying baking soda to the pan to extinguish its flames, the thought crossed her mind to just let it burn and take the shack with it. She decided against it as she didn't know for sure if the Sheriff would indeed return for her. She discarded the burnt food, no longer feeling compelled to finish cooking supper; she sat.

Sitting at the table, waiting for the inevitable beating, she watched for her father through the back screen door. Returning with his head hung down; his voice was barely audible as he informed her Leroy was dead. She had never seen him with much emotion, and even though it was slight, there it was.

"Everything is gone, completely leveled when the kettles exploded."

Beatrice couldn't be sure if he was concerned for Leroy or the fact his business was gone. He looked up from where he stood, and seeing the uncooked food, he said,

"You're worthless. And now all that mattered to me is gone."

Again, she questioned silently to herself whether it was Leroy or his stills.

Edgar walked towards the truck to retrieve a jug filled with his finest brew; lifting one from where it lay on the ground, he took a sip. He returned to the shack, where he promptly sat down in his chair at the table and began to drink, slow, small sips at first. As the alcohol started moving through his veins, the sips became gulps. Beatrice watched this act in surprise, as he had never allowed anyone to bring spirits into the house. The gulps were more intense and deliberate; the container finally surrendered its last bit of liquid. Edgar's head began swaying to and fro; his eyes were wide open, looking around the room, attempting to focus on something. With a loud burst of expletives, his head slammed onto the table, taking him into unconsciousness. Beatrice took this welcome opportunity to retreat to her bed; she was tired from the chaos of the day. She left the uncooked food on the table while the fire slowly faded, the embers providing a warm glow for her to look at while falling asleep.

The next morning, she lay in bed watching her father, who was still passed out at the table. Many questions ran through her mind. Would her dad make the trip to town? If he didn't, how would she sneak out? Leaving her bed, she began her daily chores merely out of habit. She was becoming anxious as the time to go was creeping near; her anticipation of the future created angst deep in her soul.

Edgar finally awoke from his drunken binge, stood up, walked to the porch, and took a piss in the front yard. Returning to his chair, he demanded she prepare him some food. Beatrice obeyed. When he finished scarfing up the eggs and toast she had prepared, he walked to his bed and fell fast asleep. Beatrice crept around the shack very quietly, doing as little as necessary to avoid waking him. If he remained asleep, she would quietly sneak out the back door and find the Sheriff when it was time. Just before sunset, Edgar awoke from his deep sleep. Stumbling around the room, pushing through the hangover, he attempted to dress in his best city clothes. His attire indicated he was heading out for his deliveries, bringing Beatrice a great sigh of relief. He walked out the back door of the shack while announcing he would be back tomorrow.

Beatrice was elated; Edgar was off to make his deliveries and out of her way. She didn't know if he would come back the next day or not, and frankly, she didn't care as she planned not to be waiting for him. Just go so I can start my new life was on the edge of her tongue. After he was clearly down the dirt road and she could no longer hear the whir of his tires working their way through the sandy loam, she exited the house following her known path through the woods, thankful for the full moon lighting her way to say her goodbyes.

As she approached the graves, she noticed fresh dirt had been turned between the headstones. Only a small mound of earth, not deep enough to retrieve remains, but more soil than an opossum or dog would overturn. She continued towards the pile of dirt, approaching cautiously, looking all around for signs of life. Alas, no one was to be found. She got close enough to see once again flowers had been placed on the headstones, along with a metal box open and empty lying between them. She picked up the tin box, observing it thoroughly; it appeared oddly familiar, sparking a distant memory from her childhood. Why was this here? Where did it come from? Had it been buried here for a long time? If so, who dug it out of the ground? She looked towards the far side of the field to find the shadowed figure she had seen so many times before. This time was different, though; the man stopped and waved at her before disappearing deep into the forest. Beatrice stood holding the container, trembling while watching him weave his way into the forest. Her mind was racing, standing there wondering who that man could've been and how he knew about the box.

She was soon startled back to reality when a man touched her arm. It was Sheriff Turner.

"Beatrice, what are you doing here?"

When she was not at the roadside as directed, the Sheriff parked on the side of the road, and leaving the car, he quietly began his search for her. The house was dark and empty; he assumed she would be at the graves as she had been so many times before. His instincts proved true. Not knowing about Leroy, the Sheriff insisted they take a longer path to avoid the house. Beatrice followed him obediently through the woods, quietly walking with him to the car. Settling into the plush front bench seat, they drove away. While traveling down the dusty road, no words were spoken.

Realizing she had never been inside a moving car, Beatrice began to weep, a release of memories with each tear. Recollections of her suffering were released with every saline drop.

After they were far from the Arbuckle Mountains and Honey Creek was a distant memory, the Sheriff looked at Beatrice, inquiring why she was crying. Was she sad about losing her family? Was she scared of the future for her and her unborn child? She looked up at him, eyes swollen and red,

"I am sad to leave what I know."

David felt empathy for her; he had often felt that emotion before meeting his beautiful wife. He put his free hand on hers.

"Dear sweet girl, please listen to me. These words have provided me solace in times I was hurtin'. They moved me forward when I wasn't sure I could go on. My wife spoke these words to me the day we wed; she gave me this as a gift for my soul. I hope you will take it with you as a guide for your life. 'Life is a journey we are not meant to question; we must follow our hearts and know that

God has a purpose for all of us. No matter how different we may be, our hearts beat in unison. Love wholly and purely, and strength will be found."

Beatrice absorbed the words, internalizing them, writing them on her heart. Hearing him share the words of wisdom, she began to sense David Turner was different; she didn't thoroughly comprehend what that meant at the time. She just recognized his heart to be pure and his intent honest. Taking on the phrase as a mantra, she vowed to hold dear to his advice.

Love wholly and purely, and strength will be found.

As they propelled forward up the road, heading north to Oklahoma City, the tears began to subside. With each passing road marker, her heart and mind grew brighter and calmer. Riding past the outskirts of Norman, she took in the lights sitting next to the paved roads. This was all new to her; she was in awe of each new observation. Sheriff Turner, nay, now just David, drove them to a quiet little motel on the City's southern edge. Sitting in the motel courtyard, he explained to Beatrice how he had paid for the lodging for two weeks; the room was for her to stay in while she figured out what to do. He could help no further as he must travel on. David revealed to her his leaving the Sheriff's post and duties without a note or word to anyone. He was off to start a new life, one that represented him completely.

David showed her the room and its amenities, things Beatrice had never experienced. He explained the running hot and cold water, the indoor toilet, and the tub for bathing. She was excited to experience these modern conveniences. A door with a lock and warm air piped into the room from a hole in the wall; she was amazed. Returning to the car, David drove them to a clothing store he had spotted while driving into town. Purchasing fresh garments for each of them was much needed, clothes that were clean and appropriate for them to blend in. A soft white lace-trimmed blouse, navy blue skirt with bright white socks, and saddle oxfords for her. David chose a smart set of flat-front khaki pants, a white tee shirt worn under a bright blue and white gingham long-sleeved shirt, topped off with a brown leather jacket with silver snaps matching the coat's zipper. After he paid the clerk, he asked if they could change before leaving. He disappeared into the changing room and returned a new man. Beatrice joined him at the front door, her shoes untied. David knelt down to tie them, smiling to himself as he concluded she probably had never had shoes on her feet before. He was proud she had them on correctly; right foot, right shoe, left foot, left shoe. Returning to the motel, David parked at the diner beside it. Finding a booth by the front glass, they sat down to enjoy a sumptuous meal prepared by someone else for a change.

"Here's some money for food and whatever you might need. Keep it safe and out of view from others. Should anyone ask, you will need to tell them your husband has disappeared and you haven't seen or heard from him in days. If suspected of being a single mother at your age, they will send you to a home. Be smart and cunning; you must trust your instincts."

Along with the shoes, money was a novelty to Beatrice. Soon to leave her behind and move on with his life, it was in that small diner the two of them enjoyed their last supper together. David paid the bill and walked her back to her room. Handing her the key, he told her not to open the door for anyone. The motel manager had been instructed to not enter the room without David being present; he felt confident this would ensure her privacy. David turned to leave; heading back to the car, he reminded her,

"You have fourteen days to figure out your next move; I have faith that you will be amazing."

Walking across the motel parking lot towards the diner, he heard footsteps coming toward him at a rapid pace. When he was just a few feet away from the car, he turned just as she reached him. Wrapping her arms tightly around him, she hugged him deep and hard. He received this gift of love openly and willingly. After a few moments of being embraced, she released him. David stared into Bea's eyes as they shared a tear.

"I will tell you a secret only one other person in my adult life ever knew. I, too, was forced by a man to participate in unwanted sex. I was nine years old when this happened. It was not until I met my wife that I realized I had been a victim. The man who raped me took advantage of me and my youth. He robbed me of my purity and my dignity. Ida helped me realize none of this was my fault. Remember, you, too, are a victim but do not let it define you. Don't hide the experience; use it as a tool to build a life far greater than you have ever imagined."

David Turner gave Beatrice the second-greatest gift of her life with those words. She walked the short distance back to the room, opened the door, and turned to wave goodbye. He returned the wave, and with that simple gesture, he was gone.

Beatrice awoke early the next morning, anxious as she knew she needed to quickly learn her way around town. She did her best to tie her new shoes and dress herself the same as the night before. Setting out on foot, Beatrice soon discovered a bus stop near the motel. She stood quietly at the corner, observing the people getting on and riding away. With no clue where the bus was going, she walked up the stairwell to enter the next bus when it appeared. She told the driver she was new in town and didn't understand how it all worked. Explaining the fee and where the bus was going, he took a coin from her hand and showed her how to drop it in the pay slot. Taking a seat near the front door, she paid close attention to every detail, how people got on and off, where it went, and how they returned to where they had started. Completing the route's loop, the bus driver pointed out the stop for the diner where her journey had begun that morning. Observing everything quickly and searching for answers to survival, she felt she had accomplished a monumental task that day. The concern growing in her mind was that she knew nothing of money or how to manage it.

Furthering her concern, the dollar bills David had given her were taken and replaced with coins that afternoon when she ate at the diner. The waitress who served her was very kind and gentle; as a young working girl from the country herself, she sensed Beatrice needed some guidance. The waitress asked Beatrice to have breakfast with her the next morning at the diner. She told Beatrice she would explain how a dollar consisted of one hundred pennies and how to match prices to money. Beatrice excitedly met the young woman and was quick to understand the concept and correlate the prices on the menu to what she needed to pay. Every morning she ate her breakfast at the diner before she set out on the first bus to arrive at the stop.

Riding the bus in circles every day, she encountered several lovely women on the bus asking her where her husband was; she always responded he was at work. The question was asked on one occasion where her ring was; she replied they were too poor to buy one. The response was met with a nod of understanding and appreciation for her honesty. Learning she could transfer from one bus to another without any additional expense, her exposure to the city grew. As the days quickly passed, Beatrice was becoming concerned her dollar bills were lessoning much faster than she had anticipated. The money David left her was almost gone, with only two days remaining for the room.

On her next to last day at the motel, she was on her evening bus ride heading back to her temporary residence. As she took her seat on the final bus needed to return to the motel, a woman who had been observing her for several days approached. Beatrice had been entirely unaware of the woman watching her interactions with the other women on the bus. This stranger remembered all too well how these seemingly caring people treated her as a young pregnant woman. The woman walked down the aisle of the moving bus, sitting next to Beatrice; she smiled sweetly at her.

"You have no place to go, do you? No money, no husband or home. I am just guessing, dear. No judgment, just an observation."

Beatrice looked down at the floor, scared and ashamed.

"This is my stop, dear. Come with me, and let's see if we can figure out what to do next."

The woman spoke firmly with a maternal command, compelling Beatrice to follow her.

Beatrice couldn't explain the need to follow this woman; silently, she prayed this stranger was another angel on earth.

Exiting the bus, they walked up the main street before making a turn on a lovely long road lined with a canopy of oak trees. A simple sidewalk led to the front door of a small white clapboard house. Arriving at the stoop of the simple house, the woman she followed from the bus swung the door open, inviting Beatrice to enter. A pristine home of carpets and drapes, furniture with stuffed pillows, everything clean and free of dirt. Beatrice was in awe; this was undoubtedly a step up from the little motel where she currently resided.

The woman closed the door behind Beatrice, looked at her watch, and proceeded to close the drapes, inspecting every pleat, ensuring it was correctly folded and in its place. Upon completion of her ritual, she smiled and spoke,

"Welcome, dear."

Chapter 10

Beatrice was showing quite nicely by the time she reached her fifth month of pregnancy. Having never seen a doctor or visited a medical facility before, she was quite nervous about her first visit, but Mary was insistent she visit a doctor. Beatrice was surprised by how clean and perfect everything was; the staff in their clean white pressed uniforms and pristine white shoes, even the hallways shiny and polished. It was a bit overwhelming for her at first, but she handled it with an amazing amount of grace. Mary had taken great care to find a doctor who would care for Beatrice without asking too many questions. In her search for the right doctor, Mary made a quick journey beyond the edge of town. She paid a visit to the woman who saved her from her mother, seeking her guidance in this delicate situation.

Mrs. Simpson, long since retired from nursing, was in ill health and rarely received visitors. Mary felt odd reaching out to her after so many years of being absent but was confident her dear friend would understand. When Mrs. Simpson warned Mary not to marry Thadeus, Mary walked away from the relationship she had built with the woman. She regretted that decision almost every day.

Receiving a call from Mary requesting time with her, Mrs. Simpson was delighted to hear from her estranged adopted child and asked she come as soon as possible. Shortly after arriving, Mary understood the urgency of the request. She concluded her dear friend would not remain on earth very much longer. Mrs. Simpson was gracious and forgiving, the same on her deathbed as she had been in life. Mary explained the events leading up to this young girl coming into her care as best she knew it. Hearing the details and knowing how deeply this emotionally impacted Mary, Mrs. Simpson took up pen and paper to prepare a personal note that Mary was to deliver to a Doctor Mills. A requirement from Mrs. Simpson was that Mary must not open the envelope to read the contents within. Upon confirmation from Mary to honor the conditions, the sealed envelope was handed over to Mary by the dying woman. Taking the envelope in her hand, Mary vowed to honor the request made by her savior.

On the day of the appointment, Mary made sure she and Beatrice arrived at the clinic fifteen minutes prior to the appointment time. When Dr. Mills entered the room,

Mary quickly handed him the unopened envelope; he read its contents slowly and silently, never once looking up from the letter at his guests. When finished, Dr. Mills returned the letter and its contents to the envelope. Folding the correspondence in half, he placed it in his pocket. It was then he looked up and smiled at the two of them.

"Now, Mrs. Johnson, how long has your niece been visiting with you?"

Mary was quick on the draw, responding,

"Only a few days now. She is from a small town without medical facilities; we thought it best to have her nearby. You came highly recommended to us by a dear friend."

Dr. Mills acknowledged the statement with a half-smile and requested Mary leave them alone while he examined Beatrice and the baby. Mary quietly retreated to the waiting room where she sat, nervous on the inside, cold and hard on the outside.

Mary became lost in thought, recalling two weeks before when she brought Beatrice home with her. She was prepared to have the fight of her life with her husband on taking this girl in. When Thadeus pulled into the driveway of his home that evening, Mary requested Beatrice wait on the front porch swing while the couple discussed a few private matters. Sitting in the cool evening air, she heard the side kitchen door close and the ensuing loud discussion coming from inside the house. Silently Beatrice sat swaying back and forth on the hanging wooden loveseat while the couple inside discussed her fate. Several minutes passed, and she could no longer hear what was being said in the house. A few moments more passed when the front door opened. Standing on its threshold was a man she instantly recognized. Her flight response engaged; she knew she must flee as quickly as possible.

Thadeus recalled the young girl on his porch from Edgar's place; she was the mirage girl. The two of them looked into each other's eyes, he with a stunned gaze and she a frightful squint. Thadeus' inquisitive nature automatically triggered; what had really happened down on Honey Creek that produced this young girl to his stoop?

After the gregarious argument with his wife, he intended to tell the young girl to go away and not bother them again. Upon seeing it was Beatrice, he concluded the world she came from was less than pleasant. He acknowledged his wife's unrealized connection to her.

Thadeus never knew where Mary had disappeared after the incident in Simpson's Department Store when they were teenagers. He returned to her apartment a few times in an attempt to find her with no success; she was gone. Never questioning what happened in the seven years they were apart from each other; he believed it best he did not know. The memories of Mary being young and scared when he took her home and the awful man threatening him were forefront in his mind; the memory softened his heart instantaneously. He invited Beatrice inside.

She was naturally hesitant at first, fearing he would take her back to her father. If she ran now, she might be able to get away from him. She quickly stood, turning to go. As she began up the sidewalk to the street, he bolted past the screen door. Leaving the porch, he gently grabbed her by the arm.

"The only cost for you to stay is to never tell my wife you know me or where you are from. Your father has not been seen since his last delivery. Rumor around Honey Creek is he killed the sheriff for blowing up his stills. I imagine he has run far away with that brother of yours."

Beatrice soaked the information up, pondering each scenario he offered as she knew they were all false. The mystery of what had happened to her father remained. She didn't want to know or care; she only wanted confirmation that he would never find her. With the stills destroyed, it would be months before he could re-establish the business if he indeed would.

The next words Thadeus spoke stung her deeply.

"I never knew what he did with all that money he made. He sure as hell didn't spend it on you or your brother."

She processed this information imparted; it created a feeling of sadness and self-loathing. Then she recalled what David Turner said; she had been a victim. She would not be defined by her past.

Thadeus released his grip on her bicep, replacing it with a gentle touch to her forearm. With that, she relented her escape and allowed him to escort her into the house.

Mary patiently sat at the kitchen table, mad as she had ever been. Hearing the front door close, she looked up at him, prepared to give him another scolding. From the kitchen table, looking through the doorway to the living room, Mary saw Beatrice in tow; her anger immediately melted seeing the young pregnant girl in her house. She smiled. This was an indication to Thadeus that he had made the right choice. Perhaps this would bring joy to his beautiful wife; maybe there was still hope for happiness in their home.

"Mrs. Johnson…Mrs. Johnson!"

The nurse calling her name snapped her back to the present moment.

"Dr. Mills would like to speak with you and your niece in his office."

As she walked down the hall to his office, where her young ward had been escorted, she wondered what had been in the note from Mrs. Simpson. What compelled this man to knowingly take this case, in consideration of the fact he most likely knew the circumstances presented to be a lie? Mary would never know the truth, for on that very same day, Mrs. Simpson left for her eternal adventure.

Mary took the seat next to Beatrice. Placing the young girls trembling digits in her hand, she perceived Beatrice preoccupied with worry.

"Are you doin' all right, dear?"

Beatrice confided in Mary how strange it all was. The placing of cold pieces of metal in her and a stick used to rub her insides.

Mary had never seen a doctor since her last experience and assumed this was normal, or Mrs. Simpson would not have sent them there.

"This is part of their job, dear. They are checking on you and the baby to make sure you are both well and safe. Don't worry, my sweet."

She spoke with a mother's love as she stroked Beatrice's hand.

Dr. Mills entered his office from a door adjoining an examining room, closing the door behind him. Sitting down in his oversized burgundy leather chair, he spoke across the large oak desk between them.

Looking at Beatrice, Dr. Mills made sure he had her attention before speaking.

"Everything looks good. The baby's heartbeat is strong; all indications suggest the baby is also sitting in a good position. Based on the measurements and tests run today, you are approximately five months along. We need you to eat healthy meals with lots of meat and vegetables. It is essential as you are currently a little anemic."

Mary assured him she would be well cared for from now on. Dr. Mills shook his head in agreement. Speaking to Beatrice, he asked her to wait outside while he finished up a few details with Mrs. Johnson. The doctor pushed a button on his desk, calling for a nurse; Beatrice rose from where she had been sitting next to Mary and left the room. Once in the hallway, the nurse guided her to the front waiting area, where she was to sit and wait.

"I am concerned about the girl. Her vagina and anus have been mutilated by forced entry. I trust Mrs. Simpson to always be insightful to those needing help, but I have to question if this abuse is happening in your house."

He sat there looking at Mary directly in the eye, waiting for a response. The discussion of rape had triggered Mary, bringing up deeply hidden feelings of hate for what her mother and stepfather did to her. Sitting there, she vowed to herself she would help this young girl no matter the cost. She knew her husband would never harm Beatrice and was somewhat insulted at the insinuation.

"The man who did this is dead and is no longer a concern."

Mary didn't know this to be true but felt it essential to alleviate the physician's concern.

"My husband is of no concern to her well—-"

Before she could finish, Dr. Mills interrupted her,

"I know who your husband is, which is one of my concerns."

This caught Mary entirely off guard; how did Dr. Mills know who Thadeus was?

"I give you my word; no harm will come to her while I am watching over her. I don't know what you know of my husband, but he will do as I say in my house."

Mary's confident retort led the good doctor to believe what she said to be true. He proceeded to write down dietary instructions for the young girl. After thoroughly reviewing the list with Mary, he asked her to bring the young girl back in four weeks for a follow-up.

In the weeks and months that followed, Beatrice learned what it was like to have a mother. Someone to brush her hair and cook meals, all done with love to make sure she was healthy and happy. Mary provided the same kindness to Beatrice Sarah had given her. She made Beatrice beautiful clothes to wear, the likes of which Beatrice had never seen. She created beautiful outfits for the baby with coordinating fabrics of cotton in either pure white or light yellow.

They attended Dr. Mill's appointments as scheduled; the pregnancy progressed as expected. The people who encountered Mary on a regular basis saw a woman blossoming. Lottie Bell and Herbert were thrilled to see Mary smiling and serving the customers with a lilt in her step. Thadeus found himself staying at home more and more with the two of them. He enjoyed this unintended family, the one he had secretly hoped for but never believed he could have. Thadeus began contemplating the need to alter his life and leave certain things behind. Unknown ugly secrets would create havoc for this family if he weren't cautious.

It was early in the morning on April 1, 1937, when Mary awakened to the sound of glass breaking in the kitchen. She leaped from the bed, frightened by the noise. She rushed into the kitchen to discover Beatrice on the floor, curled up in a fetal position, writhing in pain. Mary assumed this was a sign that Beatrice was about to give birth. She had never been around anyone having a baby, so she didn't know for sure but was confident they needed help. She helped Beatrice off the floor into a kitchen chair, hurriedly cleaning up the broken glass and water on the floor. Her maternal instinct and her obsession with cleanliness battled to decide what should be resolved first. The winner was her obsession; the floor received its attention before she focused on Beatrice. The pain subsided enough for Beatrice to stand semi-upright; she moved slowly down the hallway, intent on returning to her bed. Mary resolved the kitchen mess to sufficiently satisfy her demons; she then called out to Beatrice as she headed to the bathroom to prepare herself.

"Lie down and rest while I get ready, Bea. We will go to the hospital shortly."

In record time, Mary was dressed with full hair and make-up completed when she entered Beatrice's room. Assisting the pregnant girl into her clothes, they were both dressed and ready to go to the hospital. Suitcase in hand, they walked into the kitchen only for Mary to realize her husband wasn't home. The hour of the morning would make the trip difficult without the use of a car. The frequency of the contractions increased, as did Mary's anxiety while attempting to plan their journey. The bus was too far away and would not run for another two hours. There was no car available, never mind she didn't know how to drive. Mary cursed out loud at her husband for not being home. In the chaos, she hadn't noticed him pulling into their driveway.

Climbing out of the driver's seat, Thadeus heard the screams of the labor coming from inside the house. With three leaps, he was through the kitchen door, quickly assessing the situation. Taking a deep breath, he composed himself before telling Mary to grab some old blankets to cover the car seats. Mary quickly retrieved old quilts from the linen closet; rushing out the side door, she promptly covered the car seats as directed by her husband. Thadeus knelt beside Beatrice's chair and placed his arms under her legs and around her shoulders. Lifting her, he began moving towards the kitchen door leading to the driveway. Mary had returned just in time to hold the kitchen door open as Thadeus carried the panicked mother-to-be from the house. Mary assisted Thadeus in loading Beatrice into the car, crawling in the backseat next to her for moral support. Off to the hospital they went.

Arriving at St. Anthony's, Beatrice was quickly escorted to a room to wait for her doctor to arrive. She was given sedatives to lessen the pain and calm her. Beatrice's contractions continued throughout the morning; the time apart remained the same for several hours. The sedation given to her had relaxed her too much. The medicines had slowed the dilation process significantly. When Dr. Mills arrived to examine her mid-morning, he found the baby had not fully turned for a vaginal delivery. Deciding the best course of action was to give her a few more hours receiving the sedatives to keep the birth at bay. He advised that taking her into surgery to retrieve the baby would be a last resort. Concern wore its ugly path across each of the Johnsons' foreheads.

Two hours, three hours, five hours passed. Dr. Mills ordered the pain medication dosage reduced; the baby had finally moved into a suitable position for a vaginal delivery. The family members were weary by that evening, wondering how long this process would take. How much could the baby and mother endure? The reduction in the medication did not progress the delivery as the doctor had expected. At around eight o'clock, Dr. Mills announced that he felt reasonably sure all that was needed now was time. He told Thadeus and Mary they need not worry and should go home to rest; he didn't expect her to deliver that evening.

"The baby's heartbeat is strong; nature just needs a little more time."

After a brief discussion between Thadeus and his wife, Mary kissed Beatrice on the forehead. Each of them, saying goodnight, left the delivery ward for their journey home. The drive home was silent between the husband and wife, merely out of fear of what might be said. Mary unexpectedly slid her hand across the seat, placing it on top of her husband's hand. This was unexpected by Thadeus.

"Thanks."

Both of the eager pseudo-parents arose early on the second of April, anxious to return to the hospital. By 7:15 a.m., they were entering the room where they had left Beatrice the night before. She was not there. The room was clean and sterilized, waiting for the next patient. Mary immediately went into panic mode.

"What could have happened? I couldn't stand to lose another!"

She turned around, weeping she fell into her husband's arms. It was at that moment Thadeus knew he had to transform his life. He had been married to this woman whom he knew so little about for years; he never bothered to ask what had happened to the baby when they were both so young. He knew this wasn't the time to ask and quietly held her while she sobbed. A nurse in the hallway heard the crying and rushed in to find the Johnsons huddled together. She quickly inquired what was wrong. Thadeus looked over his wife's shoulder and asked what happened to the girl who was in bed last night. With a lovely lilting Gaelic accent, the nurse smiled and advised she was upstairs near the nursery.

"The baby boy was born at 2:17 this morning. Mother and baby are doing fine. Now dry your eyes, dear, and go on up the stairs to see them."

As the realization materialized that all was well, Mary kissed her husband gently on the lips.

"Thank you for being here; I have never needed you more."

Together they bounded up the stairs to find mother and child resting peacefully. Beatrice looked up through sleepy eyes to see the joyful couple enter the room.

"He is perfect—ten fingers, ten toes, two beautiful eyes, and a head full of hair."

Mary slowly neared the edge of the bed, reaching the side rails; she reached out and stroked Bea's forehead.

"I named him Kenneth. He is done feeding. Would you like to hold him?"

Mary gently lifted him up and away from his mother, pulling him tightly to her bosom. Dancing a familiar waltz around the room just as she had done with her father, she hummed Waltz Brilliance as if she had only heard it moments before. She completed her final twirl, landing in the rocking chair by the window, where they would remain entwined until he hungered again. A bond was made in this moment, a connection that would never be broken.

As she gently rocked him back and forth, Mary chanted into his ear,

"You and I will spend our lives dancing together."

Thadeus watched his wife holding the baby and immediately knew he had a problem or two.

Kenneth's first year on earth was full of changes. The Johnsons purchased beautiful furniture for the baby, re-arranging Beatrice's small bedroom to accommodate the bassinet. They treated Baby and Beatrice as if they were indeed their own. At the market or on the bus, people would ask how old Mary's children were. People assumed Beatrice and Kenneth were brother and sister; this bothered Beatrice, but she didn't contradict it. This lie continued to provide cover for her and the baby, just in case anyone might know her dad.

Mary was the consummate mother figure, providing constant emotional support for all. Taking on the role of a teacher as well, Mary began to teach Beatrice the three R's. The schooling Mary acquired as a young girl was regurgitated for Beatrice, furthering what she had learned on the farm. Misunderstandings of grammar or phrasing were corrected, furthering the distance from that little girl in the country. Beatrice was a brilliant student; she managed to cover several years of education in that one year. She picked things up quickly, giving Mary a great sense of pride as her tutor. It was as if this was the child she had lost, now returned.

Beatrice was soon upon her sixteenth birthday; her interest in boys was growing at an alarming rate, and Mary was becoming concerned. Mary had not experienced the effect of teenage hormones and didn't understand this physical attraction Beatrice spoke of. Mary was quick to discourage the behavior as she didn't want Beatrice to meet a man for fear she would go away and take Kenneth with her. She wanted her family to stay intact, exactly as it was. Thadeus recognized this was a fantasy that would not be. He was confident Beatrice would eventually fall in love and want to build a life all her own. She was a lovely young girl, simple and endearing. Her demeanor and kindness were unparalleled. Thadeus believed this innocence would lure men to her.

It was in June later that year when Beatrice brought her secret beau home to meet the family. Private First Class Torrez was a young cadet in the army, fresh out of boot camp. He was short for an army man, surprisingly just barely tall enough to be enlisted, but oh so handsome nonetheless. He had a sweetness about him that made it effortless to fall in love with him. For Beatrice, the final seal placed on their love occurred one afternoon while they were eating lunch; she revealed the truth about being an unwed mother and how it all came to pass. Tom assured her he loved her no matter what her past was and promised to protect her for the rest of his life. It was at this moment she knew David was right.

Beatrice knew she couldn't tell her adopted family she planned to marry her new love; she believed Mary would forbid it and create unnecessary chaos for all of them. Having borne witness to Mary's eccentric patterns and her overreactive behavior when she didn't like something, Beatrice decided it best only to announce their marriage after they had eloped.

It was over breakfast one morning the following July she announced the nuptials had occurred the day before. She immediately followed up with news the honeymooners would be moving to New York within the week. They were to settle there for Tom's next round of military training. In hearing the news, Thadeus expected Mary to lash out. He was full of surprise at her genteel response.

"That's perfectly lovely, my sweet. I suggest you and Tom head off to New York and get settled. Come back for

Kenneth when your house is prepared. He is too young to make that long trip, and it would make everything so much easier for the two of you. You know how much I adore each of you. He will be well taken good care of until you return."

Beatrice thought about the offer, telling Mary she would discuss it with Tom that afternoon and let her know. Tom did not like the idea of leaving the baby behind. His sense was they would survive just fine as many others before had managed similar situations, his argument valid, but Beatrice was torn with guilt as to what to do. She wanted to make things as simple as possible, knowing Mary would be lonely with the baby gone and realizing she would be in the middle of everything new trying to figure it all out; it made sense to her to leave Kenneth in the home he currently knew. Beatrice avoided announcing her decision to anyone until the day they were to board the train for New York. As Tom loaded her suitcase into the taxi, she announced to everyone that Mary should care for the baby while they were getting settled.

Six weeks passed before Beatrice returned to Oklahoma City to fetch her son; she missed him so much and couldn't wait to tell her adopted family of all the amazing things she saw in New York. A telegram was sent in advance, letting the Johnsons know when she would arrive by train. Beatrice expected the family would be anxiously awaiting to greet her on the platform; her heart sank upon her arrival in the City to find no one was there to welcome her. She stood on the platform by the train, wondering where they might be; she remained beside the Pullman cars until everyone had cleared. The train whistle blew as it pulled away from the platform, continuing to its next destination.

Just as the platform had become empty and lonely, so had her heart. Had her message not arrived? She assured herself that must be it. Quickly Beatrice walked through the station, suitcase, and purse in hand, looking for a taxi. This was to be the longest taxi ride of her life. Heading through town, towards the street where she had spent the last seventeen months of her life, it all looked the same to her. Nothing appeared to have changed; even the cars all looked the same. She recognized everything as if she had left yesterday. As the taxi pulled up in front of the house, she expelled a sigh of relief, seeing the familiar family car in the driveway. It had all been a mistake. Paying the driver his fare before grabbing her bags, she exited the vehicle and bounded up the walk towards the front door she had passed through so many times before. As she reached to grab the doorknob to enter, she was thrilled with the anticipation of seeing her son. As she turned the knob, the door didn't budge. She pushed harder only to realize it was locked. She recalled how Mary would often lock the door to keep Kenneth in the house; she knocked very gently to not startle anyone.

"Mary, Thadeus. Mary, Thadeus!"

Eventually, she observed a man's figure walking through the living room towards the front door. The door opened; she stepped back in shock as the man in the doorway was not Thadeus. Dismay ran through her, feeling the same flight response she had the first day she stood on that porch with a man in the doorway. She did not know this man; she had no clue who he was. She quickly asked where Kenneth and Mary were. Where had they gone?

The man in the doorway responded,

"I don't know who you are talking about; we just bought the house and moved in last week. The previous owner was long gone before we bought the place. The real estate agent said the people who lived here moved away suddenly and left no forwarding address."

Beatrice was in shock, the information flowing over her without any retention. Her head was reeling in disbelief at the news being delivered to her.

"We bought everything, lock, stock, and barrel. Even the car. The money we paid for it all went to support the local orphanage."

Without saying a word to the man in the door, she turned back to the street, walking helplessly away. She stopped at the curb, looking around.

"What cruel joke is this?"

She ran to a neighbor's house, asking if they knew where the Johnson family had gone. House after house repeated the same information; no one knew anything.

How could this be? Where was her son? As she walked down the street, her body numb from the information just received, she processed possible scenarios in her head. Did something go wrong between Mary and Thadeus? Had Edgar been lying in wait and taken Kenneth? Had she misread Thadeus? Should she go to the police and risk everyone finding out, she was Edgar's kid? Would her dad be able to find them?

So many secrets, so many lies, all of it overwhelming her.

Chapter 11

Business for Pretty Man was becoming a daily challenge; the day-to-day interaction with people was no longer enjoyable to him. The loss of his local, high-quality liquor supplier, combined with a constant worry for his new-found family while attempting to keep his business partners happy, created stress much more significant than he had ever known. The business had become a chore, a constant source of irritation. All this combined impacted cash flow significantly; the downgraded performance negatively affected the relationships with his partners.

Beginning in his early years of petty theft, Thadeus began hiding money that only he knew about. Over the years, enough money had been stashed outside the partnerships he could quietly disappear without altering his lifestyle. His plans never included the need to provide for a family beyond his wife; additional mouths to feed would force them to keep their lives simple. This was a minor consideration for him now; the addition to the family hooked him in a way no one could have ever predicted. With his new appreciation for Mary and a deep affection for Kenneth, he yearned for a simpler life. He was now focused on someone other than himself.

His father, unknown to him, Thadeus grew up and found his way without guidance or supervision; he figured life out on his own. His mother worked most of the time, allowing him to create his own sense of morality. All it had taken was one dare for him to begin his life as a thief; it started with petty theft from Mr. Simpson's store. This one deed opened up a world of larceny he found comfort within. Without anyone guiding his day-to-day activities, one crime led to another. The next job was a little bigger, the next one more significant than the previous one, and so on it went. Thieving came easily to him. He had charm and the ability to disarm people quickly, making it easy to take whatever he wanted from them. Occasionally, when he got caught, he would turn on his charisma and find a way out of it. He'd sheepishly apologize,

"I won't do it again, I promise!"

This seemed to always work when he flashed that winning smile while looking the recipient straight in the eye. It wasn't long before he and a couple of boys moved from petty theft to robbing banks. Somehow, they managed to always get away with their planned thievery. A little roughness was utilized if someone pushed back, but no one had ever been killed. He was grateful nothing ever escalated to the point of murder, which was odd considering the threat of death was the primary catalyst to get his point across when necessary.

With customers leaving his clubs daily due to the poor quality of the liquor, the pressure from his partners was growing. Thadeus needed to fix it, or they would fix him. The ongoing threats concerned him. He had always been able to talk his way out of problems; this time, his partners were not buying his talk, and action was demanded. Now that it was no longer just about him, he had to consider his family.

He didn't care much for the boy scout Beatrice brought home; Thadeus considered him pious and standoffish. Tom's military training left Thadeus to perceive the young suitor as always looking down on him. Thadeus often wondered if the young husband-to-be had frequented the establishments he ran. If he was a patron, Thadeus found it curious Beatrice and Tom had not discussed the clubs and their notorious owner. Perhaps Tom was not divulging his past life to her, or maybe he really was that clean-cut guy he presented. Whatever the case, Thadeus felt Tom was holding secrets back and wondered how it might impact the life he and Mary had begun to build. Even though he consciously knew Kenneth was not technically his and Mary's child, he lived his life as if Kenneth were. Thadeus believed he would be a better father than Tom. He could teach Kenneth real-life lessons.

Thadeus arose early one morning to tend to one of his clubs; leaving the house during the day was unusual and not without notice from certain people. That very same morning, Mary had unexpected guests. A couple of Pretty Man's associates stopped by to share their thoughts about her husband with her. When she opened the front door to the two very dapper men on her stoop, she could have never expected what was about to happen. Pushing the screen door open, she asked who they were looking for; pulling the screen door from her, they forced their way into her house. Quickly passing the threshold, the wooden front door closed behind them. Standing in the living room decorated to perfection, they found a surprise. On the floor sat Kenneth playing with his toys, focused on his metal miniature trucks; he had no concern with what was going on around him. The larger of the two men whisked Mary into a corner of the living room, where he constrained her. The other man sat down on the floor beside Kenneth, surrounded by his toys. He began to interact with the boy.

"My, aren't you a handsome young man?"

He coyly spoke to the child while looking up at Mary, who was pinched between her flawlessly folded drapes.

"I bet you would love to grow up and live a nice long life, wouldn't ya?"

He continued, softly and gently cooing to Kenneth. His threatening words sounded out to the pentameter of a familiar nursery rhyme.

Mary, struggling to get out of the grip the man had on her, was trapped. No matter how she tried, she just couldn't break his hold. He leaned in close to her, the fabric of their clothes meshing into one garment. He placed his tongue in the opening of her dress just above the top button, running it up her delicate fair skin; he left wet saliva trickling down her décolletage into the cracks of her breast. Years of hidden anger rocketed into action; hate boiled up to the surface, making her flesh red with heat. He moved his engorged tongue upward across her cheek, finding its way to her ear, seeking a spot to probe deeply. The point of his tongue slid into her ear canal, generating the needed spark to release her internal rage. The power of ten men filled her; she pulled a hand free from his grip and sent her perfectly manicured nails flying across his face, clawing him deep, bringing blood to the surface. He quickly grabbed her free hand and restrained her against the wall once more.

"Bad choice, dear."

Breathing heavily on her, growling, pushing his muscular body against her, he said,

"Tell your husband if he doesn't get things straightened out within a month, we will be back to take what we want."

Mary's eyes shot over to Kenneth, observing every move the man near her perceived son made.

The man sitting on the floor stood up, patting the boy on the head as he walked towards the door, motioning for the other man to follow. As the screen door closed hard against its frame, Mary tore across the room in one bound, picking up Kenneth on her way toward the kitchen. She was moving with such speed she was through the kitchen door before the men could turn. Running down the wooden stairs into the alleyway, Mary swiftly moved through the backyard gate towards the bus stop, hoping people would be waiting for their ride. She rounded the corner from the alley, going so fast that her turn took her into the middle of the street, placing her and Kenneth directly in the line of sight of a moving car. Realizing she was in danger of being hit, Mary screamed, catching the driver's attention. Quickly slamming on the brakes, the man managed to stop the car just short of Mary and the boy. Mary darted to the far side of the road to avoid being hurt, totally unaware of who was driving the car. Once on the sidewalk, she stopped long enough to see who was in the automobile. Mary peered through the side window, finding relief; it was her husband. Quickly moving to the car, she screamed hysterically,

"There were two men in our house!"

Thadeus threw the car into Park; quickly exiting the car, he left the vehicle motor purring in the middle of the street. Running down the alley towards their home as fast as his legs would take him, he passed through the gate and the yard. He pushed through the side door, searching to find these men she spoke of. Examining every room in the house, he concluded they were no longer there. He exited the house through the front door only to find the paperboy delivering papers; nothing out of the ordinary appeared anywhere in sight. Returning to where he had left his family by the car, he walked down the street in front of their home, keeping a watchful eye for anyone he might know. The car was now in sight, but

Mary was nowhere to be found. He took a moment to look around when he reached the intersection; Mary was sitting on the bus stop bench in the next block, holding the baby tightly against her.

Thadeus returned to the car, reversing it down the street to the bus stop; he collected his family. With everyone safely inside the vehicle, they proceeded home. He asked Mary to give him explicit details of the unwanted guest. Driving slowly down the street where they lived, Thadeus listened as Mary revealed the story while holding on to Kenneth so tightly he began to cry from the pain she was inflicting. Realizing she was the perpetrator of the pain, she released her grip, joining him in the shedding of tears. Parking the car in the driveway, Thadeus retrieved his wife and child from the front seat, carrying the sobbing duo into the house. Settling them at the kitchen table, he consoled each of them as he began his confession, telling his wife who he really was.

Mary took the information in, sitting there in quiet disbelief; she was hearing about the second life her husband had lived all these years. Her mind reeling from the earlier events which occurred in her own home, now this additional information left her stunned. Thadeus unfolded the stories of deceit, recounting numerous robberies, his being a gin runner in the early days, which led him to manage the clubs. He spoke about the fun the world once offered and how quickly it was all changing. He admitted it was the addition of the baby that changed his perception; what was once fun was now dangerous.

"I can't put you and Kenneth in harm's way any longer; I need to make a major alteration to our lives and leave this city, find a place where no one will know us or our past."

Allowing her time to soak up the details, he spoke with a gentle, caring tone, melting her hardcore a minute amount.

"Do you want to go with me?"

Mary sat quietly for the next hour, thinking through the information he had presented. She felt it was time for her to become vulnerable, telling him her secrets as well. With that thought, she proposed the next move.

"Make this all go away. Cover our tracks thoroughly; promise me Kenneth will never be found by his mother!"

The addition of a baby and the revealing of secret lives altered this relationship of superficial companionship to a clan with one common purpose, a grouping who needed and actually wanted each other.

The very next evening, the Johnson family sat in a car purchased quietly without any papers beyond the currency transacted. The family was making a necessary and abrupt change. Heading south to cross the state line into Texas, back to the land Mary grew up on. The contents of the Pontiac consisted of three passengers with the clothes they were wearing, an enormous amount of cash safely stored in the trunk, and hope.

Meanwhile, back in the town they left, a state judge specializing in family law opened an envelope containing $10,000.00 with a note that read:

My dear old friend, below is a list of things I need you to take care of for me. I trust the payment included is sufficient to cover costs and time. I doubt we shall ever cross paths again.

Kenneth Joseph Farrell's birth certificate is to be altered to contain the following details:

Adoptive parents:

Mother: Mary Beatrice Johnson.

Father: Thadeus Daniel Johnson.

His legal name shall be changed to:

John Edward Johnson.

As it is in all our best interests, the birth certificate should be sealed until the time of his death.

Your friend,

Pretty Man

Sequestered in his home office, the judge read the note silently. Remembering Thadeus fondly from their boyhood antics together, a smile came to his lips. He recalled the fun the two boys had while growing up together, reflecting on how their paths had taken different turns. Knowing very well secrets must stay secrets for both of them; he silently shook his head as he strolled to his private safe, where his newfound cash and its secrets were safely stored away.

Chapter 12

Mary struggled daily with how quickly time had passed; it was difficult for her to reconcile the fact John Edward had now reached four years of age. The last two and a half years had been spent moving from town to town, covering Texas from side to side and from top to bottom. They stayed in each city for as long as they were comfortable. Eventually, someone from Thadeus' past would appear and interrupt their lives by asking questions. Mary refused to return to Fort Worth. In revealing her past to her husband, he understood and never suggested they go there. Starting in Austin, as they perceived it as large enough to easily hide, they only stayed four months. Moving from Austin, southeast, to Galveston, where they stayed for a full year before moving on to San Angelo for six months. The next stop was Itasca which would only last for three weeks. They managed two months in Hogtown before finally settling in a small bedroom community where no one appeared to care who they were or what they were doing there. Ranger, Texas, had grown significantly during the oil boom of the 1920s, leaving behind a very transient community.

The area survived its sordid anti-everything past and was now composed of residents who wanted to quietly live their lives while minding their own business. This suited the Johnson family, and after only two months, they decided to make this their new home. Thadeus made arrangements to buy a house near the courthouse square. He happened upon a recently widowed man wanting to move to Los Angeles. The middle-aged man explained to Thadeus he desired to leave most of the household items behind. Thadeus thought this to be a perfect scenario as the man wouldn't be around to share the details surrounding the cash transaction with anyone. Thadeus was overly cautious to avoid unwanted attention. Should someone hear the terms of the sale, they would most certainly be asking questions he didn't want to answer. Thadeus helped the man load his truck with the possessions he wanted to take, handed him $2800, and took the deed. The items left in the house would be theirs. No buying of appliances or furniture is another success in keeping the family out of sight and out of harm's way.

The long, migratory life had been hard on Mary; her psyche took a significant hit. For a woman who was always perfect in every out-facing way, she struggled to keep up her appearance. Her hair had become long and unruly;

cutting and rolling it herself was a cumbersome task in which she lacked proficiency. Her hair color was now bland, with no natural sheen left. It had become even more difficult for her to look upon herself in the mirror, no matter how much effort she exerted. Each of them, their clothes tattered but clean, gave the impression they had little to their name. This worked in their favor as the community of approximately 5,000 people lacked excessive possessions. This trio, appearing poor, fit right into the city; no one paid them any real attention. When Mary arrived at the house, the first thing she was excited about was the sewing machine, all set up and ready to stitch new clothes. Sitting on the little back porch with large windows, the sewing room had all she needed. Mary was ecstatic that they would have new clothes again. She worked tirelessly day and night, moving as quickly as possible to settle them in a place that would finally be home.

Thadeus ventured through town on foot looking for work; his clothes, a little worn, provided the illusion he needed a job. Employment was merely a means to establish a social circle for him and his family. They didn't need the money, but he wanted the family to blend in and be a part of the community. The first job offered him, he took. A local lumber yard needed an inventory clerk to manage stock levels. The owner couldn't place his finger on it, but he sensed Thadeus knew something about supply and demand. Working in the lumber yard provided perks: minimal interaction with customers, little risk of being noticed, and a job producing the illusion he was a father working hard to provide for his lovely young family.

John Edward settled into his new surroundings almost instantly, quickly making friends with neighborhood kids. His parents never had to ask him to lie about anything; he was so young when they left Oklahoma that they were confident he didn't remember it or his birth mother.

Mary settled into the small town very quickly. People were rapidly discovering her skill for making the most beautifully adorned baby clothes; hand-woven lace incorporated with the most beautiful linen fabric was to become her signature design element. Dressing gowns for baptism and christenings were her specialty; this allowed her to command a hefty price for these specialty items. Outside of Dallas, no one else nearby was able to produce them nor match the high quality she provided. In a short amount of time, the women purchasing the beautiful garments discovered Mary was able to make dresses of equal quality for them as well. After all, it was just as important for the mother to be stunning in front of the congregation alongside her child. This was the best of all worlds for Mary; her work was recognized, and she was respected within the community. Making her own money and raising her son gave her a sense of accomplishment. This gave her great comfort no matter what the future brought. Having this business gave her the strong sense of independence she longed for. Secretly she worried what chaos might ensue; she had learned from her childhood that life could turn on a dime leaving you lost and distraught. An alternative plan, readily available, could be the difference between life and death, and she had one.

Chapter 13

For two years, Beatrice continued the search for her lost child. She traveled from New York to Oklahoma as often as possible, her sweet husband understanding her need to find her baby. Completely aware of the horrible circumstances surrounding how the baby had come to be, Tom honored her hope for finding her son. As a result of incest and rape, he secretly told himself it was probably for the best the baby was taken away. It was her brother, for God's sake, who sired the child. A sibling fertilizing an egg couldn't possibly produce a sane member of society. While training at Fort Benning, he witnessed families in the backwoods of Alabama and Georgia, where this practice was commonplace. Tom had witnessed firsthand the mental incapacitation that often occurred in the offspring. He never shared his viewpoint with his wife as he knew this would cause her great distress. Having only seen the baby a few times before they wed, he couldn't be sure but felt confident this loss had happened for a reason.

Beatrice decided to engage the police the second time she returned to Oklahoma, but since the birth certificate had been sealed by court order, she was unable to provide proof she was the mother. She also couldn't explain why the document had been sealed, and considering who the judge was that executed the order, not one person in the state would be willing to explore the possibilities of foul play. She continued her search on her own to no avail, each visit becoming more and more painful for Beatrice. Her endless quest rarely provided answers. She fully recognized the state was huge, with endless possibilities for where they could have gone, even if they had remained in the state. She also considered the fact they might have left the country. Although the odds were against her finding him, she intuitively knew her son to be alive. This maternal devotion pushed her to continue searching.

Early on, when asking neighbors if they knew anything, she received the one bit of information that kept her going. A neighbor recalled seeing a strange car parked in front of their Chrysler in the driveway one night. Curious to see who the vehicle belonged to, the nosy neighbor watched until she saw Mary carry the baby from the house to the car while her husband loaded something bulky in the trunk. She couldn't recall the car brand, only that it appeared black or dark blue. This provided enough fuel to keep Beatrice searching.

Going back and forth every few months, she continued her search. Thinking to herself it was time to give up, Beatrice returned to her east coast home once again, only to be further disappointed. Tom had received his orders; he was to be deployed overseas to France. The short amount of time they had before he left was spent together as much as possible. She loved this man deeply and feared for his safety. One month after his departure to fight in the trenches, she decided to return to Oklahoma City and turn over every rock she could find, grasping for any bit of news that would lead her to Kenneth.

Three weeks had passed since her arrival back in the City, and she was beginning to wind down. Continually hitting dead ends, running out of money, and so much time away from home was taking a physical toll on her. She was becoming concerned she might lose the husband who had been so good to her if she didn't end her quest before he returned from his tour. For some unknown reason to her, this trip seemed particularly grueling; she tired easily after the slightest exertion. A simple walk up the stairs to her room at the hotel left her breathless. Sitting on the bed in her rented room, she finally conceded to give up her search and return to New York.

Exhausted, she returned to the city streets to make her way to the train station; she would purchase a ticket home. Back at the hotel, she sat in the dining room to eat her supper. Before she ate her dinner that night, she paused and gave thanks for all she had. Returning to her room, she undressed and prepared herself for bed. Her sleep fitful that last night in Oklahoma, filled with random dreams. Visions of her father and brothers, her son playing in a field somewhere, and just before she woke, a call from her mother offering her a gift of peace. With the dream of her mother stuck in her mind, she was now fully prepared to leave this part of her life behind and return home.

Following her typical morning routine, Beatrice began to dress. While buttoning her blouse, she noted it felt a little snug; she blamed the added padding on the lousy food she had consumed over the last few weeks. Beatrice also contended she was a bit swollen from the lack of rest. Feeling slightly sluggish, she meandered down the stairs of the hotel and out of doors to the cafe across the street. She hoped a full morning meal would energize her before heading to her train. Finishing her meal and paying the bill, she proceeded back to the hotel to retrieve her bags. It was then it hit her. As her breakfast lay on the unsuspecting car tire, she traveled back in time, remembering what morning sickness felt like the last time she was pregnant. Pulling herself together, she stood up and walked away from the liquid she had deposited on the street. Leaving the hotel with luggage in hand, she decided this pregnancy supported the vision from her mother; she belonged on the East Coast with her husband and a new family. Boarding the train to begin her next adventure, she said goodbye to Oklahoma forever. Sitting in the plush velvet seats on the train, she was reminded of her conversation with Sheriff Turner; she had to move on from being a victim. Her future was to unfold far from this place.

Arriving in New York City after her three-day journey, Beatrice was tired yet full of energy; she was elated about the child on its way. Making her way through the busy New York streets from Grand Central Station, past the noisy street vendors with their carts, she headed home. The long walk from the terminal to her building downtown reminded her how much she had missed the noise and the smells of New York City. It all felt right.

Ascending the stairs to the second-floor apartment on Bleecker Street, she was greeted by two men in olive green wool suits. The stripes on their shoulders represented their importance; although she didn't know the exact significance, she knew their visit was important. Confirming she was the wife of Tom Torrez, both men removed their hats before continuing their task. The elder of the two men removed a telegram from his jacket pocket. War Department was stamped in bold above Beatrice's name. Before even opening it, Beatrice knew her husband would never return to meet the gift he had given her.

Chapter 14

It was late summer, and John Edward would soon start another school year. During the years they resided in Ranger, he had gathered a vast collection of friends who appeared to enjoy his company no matter how silly or off he acted. Adults in the town knew him well, and unfortunately, not for a good reason. He had acquired a reputation for being a prankster, nothing that ever hurt anyone too seriously. The women in town did not like their daughters being around him; they knew of the mischievous nature surrounding this boy; boys like him don't grow up to be good God-fearing husbands. Typical of summers in West Texas, August was hot and dry, the midday heat unbearable most of the time. Children were forced by their mothers out from under the swamp coolers to play out of doors most days.

Thadeus was home for lunch and would soon be headed back to work when Mary shewed John Edward outside to play with his friends; she would be away from home that afternoon. Mary asked her husband to drop her off at the beauty shop for her weekly wash and set on his way back to the lumber yard. To walk the short distance to the beauty parlor that day in the dreadful heat was more than she wanted to endure, and today she had a choice. Thadeus was happy to oblige her request; waving goodbye to John Edward, they drove the short distance down Main Street to the hairdresser's shop. Leaving her at the front steps to the salon, Thadeus smiled and waved as he returned to work at the lumber yard. Mary so enjoyed her time at the beauty shop; hearing the latest town gossip from her hairdresser was always a treat for her. She once asked if she was ever the talk of the shop; the response from her stylist was stinging.

"Honey, you and your husband are so boring; there ain't nothing to talk about! Now John Edward, on the other hand..."

Her roll-up completed, Mary sat under the scalding hot hairdryer, thoroughly enjoying the latest issue of Harper's Bizarre. The heat from the dryer was as unrelenting as the air outside. Mary pushed the dryer hood open to reach for a fan laying a few chairs down when the power to the shop went off, leaving the dryers without their familiar hum. Ladies raising the appliance's smokey grey hoods peered at one another, seeking insight.

"Bet you anything, my son had something to do with this!"

Mary bellowed out in laughter.

The ladies around her giggled, surmising it was probably true. The stylist busily checked their client's curlers in hopes someone was dry enough for a comb out; they had no idea how long it would be before the power would return. The doors of the shop were propped open in hopes a breeze would flow through. Milling about in the semi-sun-lit room, the ladies suddenly heard the loud cries of a boy running down the street.

"He's dead!"

The ladies jumped from their seats on cue, exiting the front door to stand on the sidewalk, anxiously seeking out who the victim was. As Mary exited the salon door, she saw her son being picked up off the street by two men. Her eyes followed the string in his hand up to the homemade kite now resting in the power lines. Her heart sank as she began to tremble; fear took control of her muscles, making her unable to move. Her brain signaled her legs to run to him; her feet refused to follow the order. The two men laid his body in the back of a nearby truck. John Edward was lying perfectly still; there was no movement from him, not a twitch of muscle activity. A man loudly banged on the fender of the truck, which caught Mary's attention; the signal to go had been given to the driver. The flatbed sped down Main Street, heading towards the hospital, passing directly in front of the beauty shop with its patrons on the sidewalk. Mary saw her son's lifeless body bouncing in the truck bed, flopping around like an untied bale of hay. Car keys in hand, Mary's devoted hairdresser appeared at her side.

Grabbing her, Nannette dragged Mary to the car parked just in front of them, tire tread remnants flying through the air as she released the clutch, racing to reach Mary's son. Screeching to a stop in front of the hospital steps, Mary flung the car door open, exiting swiftly. Looking to the hospital entrance, she found Thadeus standing on the steps leading to the front doors. The lumber yard foreman had witnessed the incident and contacted the shop immediately when he realized who the boy was. Attempting to run past him, Thadeus reached out his hand to grab Mary's elbow. Stopping her short of the front door, he pulled her close to him.

"Stop, don't go in there just yet. I need to tell you something. I spoke to the men who brought him here; it appears he took a direct hit of electricity through his right arm. His shoes somehow grounded him; the current flowed through his body and back to the ground out the sides of his feet."

Mary looked into her husband's eyes.

"What are you saying? Is he dead or not?"

Thadeus held back the tears in his eyes; he was attempting to explain the situation to her when a doctor appeared at the glass double doors, motioning for them to come inside.

"He is alive but has severe burns on his right arm and holes in the side of each foot where the electricity exited his body. It's a miracle he survived. We won't know for a while if there is any brain damage; I must warn you, it is quite likely he will have lost some brain tissue. His wounds are being dressed then he will be moved to a room in the burn ward. He will require complete bed rest for the next six weeks before he can go home. The pain from the burns will be constant, so be prepared for the recovery to be a slow process. It will take time for him to heal; I fear the scarring will be significant."

Hearing this news, Mary began to sob, for she knew the guilt and shame she carried due to her scars. Fearing that horrible burden for her child was insufferable. She always had been able to hide her physical scars from the world; he would not have that luxury. Knowing he would not be able to avoid the judgment this disfigurement would bring deepened her sorrow.

It seemed as though an infinity passed before the gurney carrying his charred, wounded body was wheeled into the hallway, moving toward his home for the next six weeks. John Edward was incoherent from the pain medication but woke enough to see Mary and call out,

"Mother..."

As Thadeus and Mary followed the nurses pushing the gurney through the hallway, a man exited a patient's room into the corridor. Saying his goodbyes to the room's occupant, he was oblivious to his surroundings. Exiting the room, the man bumped straight into Mary, causing her to stumble and fall to her knees on the cold hospital floor. He quickly and graciously helped her up; he continuously offered apologies for not paying attention. Reaching out his hand to Thadeus as a gesture to apologize, the two men shook hands. Recognition between the two of them was instant. Thadeus had been found.

The man slowed his handshake with Thadeus, smiling sweetly; he released his grip. He turned to exit the building, looking over his shoulder, his gaze fixated on Thadeus. Thadeus stood watching the man walk out the hospital doors, knowing full well who he was. He acknowledged to himself he had been discovered, and his family was now in danger.

With John Edward in the hospital, he would never persuade Mary to leave. It was painfully evident to Thadeus the family could no longer run.

Thadeus was buried three days later in the local cemetery.

Chapter 15

Five years after burying her husband, Mary began forming plans for her and John Edward to leave Ranger, Texas. Opportunities for her were limited, and she didn't like being viewed as the Widow Johnson. Following the guidelines her dead husband taught her, Mary looked for a buyer that could pay cash for the house. This played along with the first rule he ever taught her; the fewer questions to be answered, the better. Now that she was choosing to leave, she was forced to learn to drive, it was not without challenge or peril, but she managed. She had often observed the motions of the clutch in tandem with the shifting gears when riding with her husband, so with scratched fenders and a few mailboxes laid to rest, she somewhat mastered driving.

During her planning stage, she was sipping coffee one day at the Woolworth's counter, where Mary overheard talk about Dallas and how fashionable it was. Mention was made about a high-end department store in Dallas selling custom-made designer clothes. Her counter mates discussed how one could be measured for an exact fit of any dress in the store collection. At first, Mary wondered why this was such a big deal; her clothes were always made to fit precisely. Sitting, listening to the woman brag about this store, the idea came to her.

She convinced herself the dressing gowns she had been selling in Ranger would be very popular in Dallas. She just knew her designs would be well received in a city like Big D. The decision where they would move to had been finalized. With two dressing gowns sewn but not yet purchased, her samples for the store were already produced. Her experience in making a pitch to a store owner for her goods was well-defined and rehearsed; she had done it before. She felt good about her plan; this gave her the necessary determination to move forward.

Just as they had initially bought it, the house was left intact. Everything that was in the house when they moved in remained. She packed clothes, cash, scrapbooks, any and everything with their names on it. The car packed to capacity, and they were off to begin again. She cleverly covered their tracks to such an extent that she paid the funeral director a hefty sum of cash to purchase two additional burial plots next to her husband's. The sum was large enough to convince the funeral director to place a placard on the site next to Thadeus. *Baby Johnson* was all it said. The owner of the funeral home acquiesced with a smile and a thick wallet. With the house now sold and the plots purchased, all was set in motion. Off they went east to begin the next chapter in their lives.

Arriving in Dallas, they took up residence in a motel on Highway 80. Close to town, but far enough away to hopefully keep John Edward from finding trouble. The motel was small; Mary knew this would not be long-term, but she wanted to approach the buyers at the upscale store before making permanent living arrangements. She set up an appointment with the chief buyer at the store the very next day. Upon her arrival and display of goods, the buyer told her the stitch work was perfection, but dressing gowns for children were out of fashion. If she would bring him something more relevant to the current culture with more color, the store would most certainly buy them.

Mary left the store determined to have her clothes sold at this downtown location. Finding a fabric store on her way home, she began to comb through patterns and fabric, searching for inspiration. She recalled a magazine at the beauty shop with pictures of newborn boys dressed in light blue and girls dressed in light pink. There it was; Mary knew what to do. She purchased several yards of material in each color, a portable sewing machine, several types of notions, and thread. With her supplies in hand, she returned to her small room at the motel, where she went to work making the new designs. Two days later, she returned to the store with her new line of children's wear. The buyer was ecstatic to see the baby blue jumper with crossed straps up the back and pearl buttons on the bib. The girl's version was a pink blouse with an attached skirt and matching diaper cover to be worn underneath. He placed an order for two sets in several sizes. As they would carry the store's logo on the tags, Mary would never get credit for her creation.

With an advance from the store and the need for more space, she began searching for an apartment to rent. Buying a house would be suspicious; a single mom with a teenage son purchasing a home would create too many inquiries. She was unwilling to risk anyone finding out where they had come from. Another lesson for her from Thadeus was to stay out of other people's conversations. To rent an apartment in Dallas, proper seemed too costly; she decided they would have to look in other areas outside of downtown. With buses being quite popular, getting around the city was very simple. Even though she had learned to drive, she didn't like to. She preferred mass transportation. Within a week of searching, she obtained a suitable apartment where she and John Edward could live. It was a simple two-bedroom apartment in a suburb of Dallas, Oak Cliff, TX. The new apartment was located close enough to the school John Edward would attend; walking to and from class every day would be quite easy for him. The location was also convenient for the easy delivery of her clothing to the downtown store. For the first time since her father died, her life was becoming uncomplicated, finally allowing them to settle into a routine. With her husband out of the picture and in a new town, there was no one else to answer to and no one else's rules to follow. John Edward began attending school the following week; his performance in classes was better than Mary had expected, considering the kite incident in Ranger. She was quick to keep him close at hand and away from young girls. Knowing his interest in girls was peaking; Mary was fearful of what trouble he might get into. Mary never spoke about sex or her past to her son; there was no need for him to carry the burden of her life or the terrible mistakes she had made.

He was her reason for being; she had always done whatever was necessary to protect him. That would never change.

Returning to the apartment one October afternoon in 1953, Mary exited the bus near her home with her arms loaded with fabric. She stepped down from the vehicle and saw John Edward being pulled by the arm toward their apartment. Mary walked quickly to the building from the direction of the bus stop, calling out to ask what was going on, demanding to know what trouble her son was in. The man dragging him never loosened his grip until he and Mary were face to face. Looking her straight in the eye, Mary was stricken with an emotion she had not felt since a lifetime ago, causing her to forget all placement of time and space as she looked at this man. John Edward struggled to free himself, proclaiming he didn't have anything to do with it. Mary quickly composed herself, hiding all external signs of what she was really feeling or thinking. Very coolly, she began,

"Is he in some sort of trouble?"

The six-foot-three hulk of a man spoke in a deep, lyrical timbre.

"It is more of a matter of where he is spending his time. The boys he is running with are known hoodlums who are going to coerce him to do something that will cause both of y'all trouble. I have seen this happen way too many times; I felt I needed to give you fair warning as I understand his father to be deceased."

Mary confirmed her marital status with a single nod. John Edward observed his mother grow flush; he had never witnessed this before. Even on the rare times, she spoke of his father, this warm glow had never shown.

"May I offer you some tea or coffee?"

Mary's pose quickly shifted, one ankle bent slightly into the other, causing her still near-perfect body to suggest an initiation.

"Mr....?"

"Bennett, ma'am, Bernard Bennett."

"Please come in, and let's discuss what you think is best for him to do."

Three weeks later, Bernard and Mary were married at the Justice of the Peace in Fort Worth, Texas. Mary willingly returned to her hometown when Bernard asked her to marry him.

Bernard asked Mary very few questions about her past. Having served as an educator for over 25 years, he was quick to sum people up and felt she had a strong character. John Edward needed a strong male role model in his life, and Mary sensed Bernard would be a good influence. Bernard was committed to five more years of work before retirement; he was older than her by several years, causing her to be quite relaxed with him. She figured he would not push the notion of a sexual relationship due to the age gap between them.

Bernard owned a simple white clapboard house at the North end of Fort Worth. The simple house sat on two residential lots on top of a hill overlooking the cattle planes of the river and the city residing on top of an old fort. Mary would never speak of her former life here with him. The area had changed significantly, which minimized the likelihood anyone would now recognize her; she was content to leave that part of her life asleep. On occasion, she found herself strolling past the home that had once belonged to her grandparents. The carriage house, long since destroyed by a fire, had never been rebuilt. A group of Fort Worth debutantes started a collection to save the main house, intent on preserving its original state. Beyond the performance hall downtown bearing the family name, no one remembered what the Smiths had done for Fort Worth.

Nonetheless, a house so grand must be saved. This was the first of many rescues by the newly formed historical society. Mary would attend their public meetings when they were seeking donations for research or for purchasing additional homes. Still, for obvious reasons, she was never able to share any of her knowledge regarding the mansion. Years later, the apartment building deeded to Mary would be donated to the league anonymously.

Much to everyone's surprise, John Edward finished high school with adequate grades to receive his diploma. Daddy Bennett encouraged John Edward to attend college, knowing full well the effort was futile. He and Mary had hopes John Edward might see other parts of the world and that this would help him mature his underdeveloped mindset. It was even suggested he go to New York for a year or two.

With his high school certificate in hand, John Edward refused any further education. The military option was suggested and was agreeable to John Edward. The damage to his feet from his teenage accident made him ineligible; this bothered his mother more than him.

With that option gone and his refusal to seek higher education, his step-father insisted John Edward find a job to provide his own way. Bernard had longtime friends working the oil fields just outside Odessa, Texas. Arrangements were made for his stepson to head west to work. Most who knew John Edward thought the hard work would encourage him to return to school; the only reward for his work in West Texas was a pregnant teenage girl he would walk down the aisle.

When he and Bettie returned to Fort Worth, she was three months pregnant with their first child. Thus, the unpleasant relationship between the two women began. It would take Mary years to realize her son had a role in creating the chaotic marriage her son and daughter-in-law endured.

With every new year, another child was born, providing Mary with one more grandchild. The relationship between mother and daughter-in-law grew more strained with every birth. Mary watched the young couple struggle with finances, both husband and wife working to provide for their family. Bettie and John Edward led separate lives, working opposite shifts to make sure someone was around to care for the kids. Theirs was a marriage of convenience, for which Mary resented her daughter-in-law.

John Edward was an astute student of his mother; he observed her mental strategies and utilized them when necessary. His best-learned lesson was the 'keep smiling and pretend everything was okay.' He played the role so well that Mary didn't catch on until after the couple's divorce in the early 70's how miserable he was. It was a bitter pill to swallow to realize her daughter-in-law had been the glue keeping the marriage together.

Outside of paying constant attention to her son's life, Mary's life became rather dull. Her husband had insisted she stop working when the Dallas store refused to place her brand label on the clothing she designed and produced. She often talked about going to New York to sell her clothesline, but Bernard would have none of it. Daddy B had retired from work and wanted his wife at home with him.

During the spring of her sixty-fourth year, Mary was diagnosed with breast cancer; a double mastectomy was the treatment plan. The many years without hormones, while never seeking medical attention, had taken their toll on her body. Mary would once again face the pains of her body being altered. The breasts were removed, leaving additional scars on her body, further evidence of her body being violated. These scars were easily hidden by the use of false breasts concealed in a beautiful dress; the emotional scars, however well-hidden, never healed.

Chapter 16

Back in New York, her husband deceased, she could do nothing but push forward. This repetitive theme in her life was growing tiresome, but she was determined to not let the sadness of Tom's death negatively impact the health of the baby she was carrying. During her first doctor's visit to confirm the pregnancy, she observed the women in the office performing their assigned tasks. Typing, taking blood pressure, and checking people in for their appointment. Watching all the activity around her, it occurred to her that being literate was the only way she could afford a decent life for her unborn child. The military insurance from her husband's death provided funds enough to cover expenses through the pregnancy. Perhaps she could stretch the money beyond the child's first year if she was extremely frugal with her spending. Her early years without money to do as she saw fit had been rough; she would not put her child through that. With a commitment to the future, she began working on her General Education Development certificate. Having the equivalence of a high school diploma would at least allow her an office job. She committed almost every waking hour to her studies, with a complete focus on passing the exam. If she worked hard, she could complete the GED and start to work after the baby was born. Obtaining this goal would leave her cash for a safety net.

Her money stretched further than expected as her guardian angel paid regular visits. She relaxed a little, knowing he was still nearby; his presence was regularly confirmed by events occurring that defied explanation. One afternoon, she returned home from a doctor's visit to find the delivery boy from Mr. Pong's grocery store delivering groceries to her. She was concerned as she had not ordered anything. The items had been paid for by someone who wished to remain anonymous. She was grateful for these events, gifts pure and simple.

After the baby was born, another act of kindness occurred; her apartment rent for several months was paid in full by Mr. Anonymous. When the landlord gave her the news, she begged him to tell her who the generous person was. Through his heavy Puerto Rican accent, Señor Estefan explained how an envelope with cash had been placed under his door that morning. Instructions were typed out on a piece of paper, specifically named Beatrice, and included her apartment number. The money accompanying the directive was sufficient to cover her rent for the next twelve months. Señor Estefan, concerned about where the bills had come from, clearly stated he had counted it twice, just to be sure.

Again she had no idea who it was or why they did it but was forever thankful for the kindness shared. It was with this gift that she decided to seek a higher level of learning; she began her search for enlightenment. She was compelled to explore opportunities allowing her to give back, just as she had received. Having completed her GED with a near-perfect score, she began her search for a school of higher education, exploring different courses of study and reading all she could.

She continually, whether subconsciously or not, found books addressing the subject of rape. A victim of rape herself, she was intrigued by the information occupying the pages. This new knowledge provided her with a means for releasing her past demons. This exploration and release created a desire to befriend others who had been victims of unwanted aggression. Continuing with the research of psyche and fact, she chose to pursue work in the field of psychology. Her heart told her she was on the right path; her focus never wavered as she applied to Barnard College; she was accepted and would begin classes the following fall term. The first year of school was tough, but she managed quite well. As a scholarship recipient receiving funds for tuition and books, she was set for the year.

Beatrice focused on the present; worry was not a luxury she had time for; the future would be addressed when necessary. The school offered a work-study program explicitly designed to assist widows of the war; she utilized this service to land a job as a professor's assistant in the psychology department. This provided her with additional resources and insight into the field she planned to work in. The young woman who lived next to her, also widowed, worked opposite hours of Beatrice's school obligations. They agreed to trade off childcare, saving each of them money and giving them solace that their child would be well cared for. Trusting someone with her child again was a healing moment for Beatrice. She held on to her faith, pushing through the fear.

During her third year of studies, she began to uncover information indicating rape to be more common than she had imagined. Boys, girls, siblings, priests, pastors, school teachers, perpetrators, and victims existed in all these categories. Discovering how deeply people hid their shame, she was horrified at how they chose to mask their pain: gluttony, self-deprecation, alcoholism, hedonism, and the saddest of all to her — suicide. Her extensive research generated a long list noting how people acted out. More often than not, the perpetrator of the violent act was in a position of control; they had power over the victim in some way. Often threatening to ruin the victim's life at the perpetrator's whim. Beatrice remembered Leroy threatening her if she spoke out. She concluded this was a common part of the violence, fear-mongering in its most heinous form. During her discoveries, Beatrice met several young men who had been defiled by men with varying forms of deprecation, often performed by family members or clergy. She was appalled to learn the number of boys raped was at par with the number of young women. When talking with these young men, she would tell them the story David shared with her on the road while escaping their personal prisons. She always repeated David's advice not to be defined by remaining a victim.

Beatrice became resolute in her dedication to giving victims a voice and allowing them to speak and be heard. She wanted a safe place where they could express their pain and, hopefully, find a resolution to their shame. She was vigilant in helping them find a path to remove the guilt they carried and let them understand they were not responsible for what had happened to them.

Her work was tireless in the city; she befriended anyone she sensed might have been a victim. Rich, poor, black, white, homosexual, heterosexual; there were no boundaries to be drawn, no overarching categories. She sought out people who were robbed of their fundamental freedom of choice, anyone who didn't get a choice as to whether they wanted to participate or not.

She completed both her bachelor's and master's degrees and continued with her studies, working toward her doctorate. Ten years came and went since the death of her beloved Tom; in the time that had passed, she pushed forward. She was driven by unseen forces opening windows and doors to take the next step, managing life the only way she knew how; by finding and following the light.

She was now ready to defend her thesis, "Victims: Healing States Through Verbalization." Her research was brilliant and well-delivered. Victims' disturbing stories had been shared with Beatrice and carefully cataloged for the sake of research. Scenarios were laid out clearly, proving those who found healing by walking through their pain and those who weren't ready to address it. Human beings are often left to endure their acts of shame. Beatrice collected countless stories of people afraid to upset their families by speaking out about what had happened to them; how this deep dark secret drove their life. Men raped by an uncle at an early age, the act of violence upon them was never known beyond them and the perpetrator. The unfortunate result would end in their decision to violate another family member. The cycle of abuse repeated over and over.

Her dissertation was challenged by the faculty chair. The professor ridiculed her hypothesis, questioned the methods chosen, and suggested she utilized the fear of these people to support her analysis.

Her final words in defending her thesis:

"We are given a voice to speak, memories both painful and joyful. The mind cannot distinguish the range of good from bad or perceive the benefits of either joy or sadness if we don't speak of both light and dark. To find balance and self-love, we simply cannot hide who we are from the world. It is our wounds, when healed that allow us to grow."

Walking proudly across the graduation ceremony stage, she received her doctorate. Her desire to lead a life with purpose and meaning was being fulfilled. All the pain delivered to her throughout the years propelled her forward, providing her with the opportunity to help others. It was surreal, and she was content; this fulfillment was a combination of all the bad and all the good in her life. After the pomp and circumstance had ended, holding her young son's hand, they walked out of the graduation ceremony. Beatrice held her head high; a new chapter in her life was beginning, and she was ready and armed.

Exiting the doors leading out into the sunlight, she was both warmed by the sun and temporarily blinded. Through the momentary lack of vision, she noticed a man blocking their path. As her pupils adjusted to the outside light, she began to recognize the soft outline of his face. Although it was a little bit worn by life, she immediately knew the blue eyes shining brightly at her. Fond memories of this man washed over her, enhancing the natural high she was on. Standing in front of her and her son was the man she had often suspected as her guardian angel, the man who kept watch over her most of her life. Moving into a rapid stride, she walked towards him with arms outstretched, longing to hold him close. Seeing him produced an overwhelming joy in her soul. He extended a hand to greet her; she moved passed it straight into an embrace. He lifted her off the ground, squeezing her tightly. Twirling around in the afternoon sun, he finally stopped and placed her back on the ground.

Releasing her hold on him, she turned to her son and said,

"I want you to meet a dear friend of ours; this is David Turner."

The child looked up at David and stretched out his hand to shake the man's hand.

Beatrice continued,

"It is so wonderful to see your smiling face. I can't thank you for all that you have done to help us through the years. Your kind deeds were so excessive, but without it, I wouldn't be here living this amazing moment."

She continued praising him, listing each of the anonymous gifts she was aware of; this acknowledgment generated a knowing and loving smile on his face. Finally, when she stopped to take a breath, David interjected that it was not he who had helped her through the years, at least not beyond their adventures together back in Oklahoma.

"I know who was lurking in the shadows of the trees when you were young, and the same amazing person has been providing for you since your husband died."

Beatrice paused momentarily and thought back to the man who waved at her from the trees that day in Carter County. She thought back to all the times she had felt this presence that she could never explain. She then connected the dots that David had been waiting in the car for her that day; he wasn't the man in the trees.

From behind her, she heard a voice that took her back to when she was four years old. The last time he spoke to her, she was standing in that old shack once called home.

"Hello, Bea!"

She spun around to seek confirmation it was who she hoped. It was her beautiful brother, Aaron. He reached for her with reckless abandon, needing to hold her. She returned to his arms, the last place she remembered him holding her. Each of them embraced their loved one tightly; the years melted away in an instant.

Brought back to reality by her son pulling on her skirt, she turned away from her brother to look down at him. Eyes red and full of tears, she lifted her son, thrusting him forward into her brother's arms.

"Aaron, please meet your Uncle Aaron."

Her son carried her dear brother's name, a remembrance of the one she thought lost so many years ago. Beatrice reached out to collect a hand from each of these two beautiful men. Younger Aaron in his uncle's arms, the foursome walked from the campus south to her apartment.

Beatrice had worked with and built friendships with several queer men during her studies at Barnard, having become a deep part of their personal lives; she developed a sixth sense for when two men were in love. Walking between David and Aaron, she now understood the connection between these two men. Why David had taken her away from the farm and provided her with a chance to start anew. David's soliloquy in the car ride north from Honey Creek, talking about the need to live a life free, the need to disappear, now all made sense.

Sitting at her kitchen table, her son tucked in bed and soundly asleep, Beatrice smiled at David.

"Did you know Aaron was alive when you took me away from Honey Creek?"

Before he could respond, she quickly turned to look at Aaron.

"Were you the one who blew up the stills, killing Leroy?"

Her lips poised to toss another question out to the two men, her brother interjected,

"I couldn't save you from what Leroy did, but I could make sure it wouldn't ever happen again. David, as did everyone else, assumed I was dead until seven years ago. I have been watching over you since I disappeared that fateful night back in Oklahoma. It was difficult to watch the struggles you had after Mom died. It was necessary I remain hidden for your safety as well as mine. The night I disappeared, I turned myself in to the Feds, agreeing to provide information on illegal brewing locations and the clubs where they were sold. Part of the agreement was that the family would be spared if I disappeared. The raid on the farm was only for show, and Leroy should not have gone to prison.

It was the following year after you arrived here in New York with Tom that I settled in the village. Experiencing life in this wonderful bohemian part of the world, I was as content as I had hoped to be. One cold November morning, while sitting enjoying coffee at my favorite deli counter, a stranger walked in and sat on the stool next to me. I paid my bill and stood to go; taking my coat from the rack; I looked back to admire the handsome man once more. As I opened the door, I took a moment to steal one last glance. Aware of my staring, he looked up at me and smiled. The moment lingered as we both real-ized we knew each other; the gaze being returned had not been present for a very long time. I put my coat back on the rack and returned to the seat next to him. Requesting another cup of coffee, I laid my hand on his knee. Without even a glance around the room, he took my hand into his. Sitting there in silence, we just held hands, taking in the moment. This instant became endless; I can still smell the food being cooked, see the stained menus and the brown beadboard on the walls, all covered with photos from the past. The emotions were so strong in each of us that no words were necessary. After our coffee cups were empty, he casually turned towards me on his counter stool, looked at me, and asked if I was ready. We have managed a beautiful life together ever since."

Aaron finished telling about the reunion of their souls; he then leaned across the table, where he gently placed his lips on David's.

Beatrice sat quietly for a few moments, observing these two men at her kitchen table. Watching the two men share a kiss, she shed a simple tear for the compassion and commitment these two men shared, a love stronger than steel.

Contemplating the twist and turns of her life, Beatrice silently acknowledged she was content. Even with the loss of her firstborn, a pain she admitted would never leave her, the love of Aaron, and the return of her brother and David, she had all she would ever need.

Chapter 17

The day that followed was filled with stories regaling the life Aaron had lived and the adventures he had been on. Some actions were done by choice; others were forced upon him in order to protect the family. He carried little remorse for the life he had lived; Aaron knew deep in his soul he had made the right decision to turn in the prohibitionists to keep his family from harm. The death of his mother, along with the babies, did, however, continue to haunt him. He often questioned if he had stayed, could he have saved them. Over time Aaron came to believe their passing was an act of God, removing his beautiful mother away from the awful day-to-day chaos and emotional pain she lived in, also as an act to save the twins from a life of abuse. He shared stories about his travels around the United States, seeking out gin mills and speakeasies to provide law enforcement with evidence. Aaron spoke of how much he actually enjoyed playing the double role. His travels took him to amazing places he never knew existed, discovering places he would have never encountered if he hadn't made the deal. When he was first introduced to New York during the second year of his new job, he developed an immediate affection for the noise and bright lights that never left him.

The theatre, all the amazing different cultures, the museums, all weaving in and around each other on that one small island. He made trips to the South whenever directions from his boss deemed it so. He had been fortunate enough to work for a kind old judge from Vermont, who befriended him early on. The old man, widowed and lonely, became a friend and mentor. These two loners became great companions, a male bond strong enough to stand the test of time and a platonic friendship that would one day prove to save his life.

When responsibilities took him west of the Mississippi River, Aaron would divert his travel through Carter County to check on Beatrice. He talked of times when he would sit outside David's house, peering through the windows at his two former lovers. His heart was full from the times they shared, and that was enough. He knew he could not reveal himself; should he be found out, the impact on all the people from his past life would be significant. He chose to spend his solitary life longing for this man, eventually earning redemption for his choice.

This pattern repeated itself, one year leading into another. Aging silently and alone, Aaron lived a happy life.

Time spent with his platonic friend, the judge, provided the emotional connection he needed. An occasional tryst with a stranger would occur, the event never leading to anything permanent due to the fact that his heart still belonged to David. Having already paid the price of losing love once, he believed the cost to be too great to love again.

Preparing for another work trip to Texas, the judge summoned his young friend for a visit. Walking through the back door of the judge's home on the Upper East Side of Manhattan, he sensed he was being followed. When he arrived, the judge told him, in confidence, he must disappear as quickly as possible. The boys had discovered Aaron's homosexuality and were plotting to kill him. There would be no tribunal, no pleas heard, only a simple lynching with no one the wiser as to what happened to a paid informant. The sweet old man said he would cover Aaron's tracks and report he had been killed on assignment. Aaron would no longer use his assigned government name, finally returning to the man he was long ago.

Being freed from his obligation to the government and the risk of impending death, he decided to return to Honey Creek and reveal himself to David and Beatrice before disappearing with them in tow. He intended to visit the graves to retrieve his tin box buried so many years back; the money stored within it would be useful for their escape. Approaching the graves from the creek, he saw Beatrice approach the burial plots. Seeing her amble in the morning sun, he observed the protrusion of her abdomen, giving him cause to reason his sister was with child. His assumptions of her being pregnant ignited a fury within him. The anger overtook him as he assumed she had been raped; he briskly headed to the stills where Leroy was.

In Leroy's drunken state, he confessed to the ghost of his half-brother standing in front of him; he was the father of the child Beatrice carried. Leroy was belligerent towards the prodigal son who had returned, threatening Aaron with a wooden log that was meant for the fire. Being inebriated, Leroy could only manage to stumble towards him before dropping the wood to the ground. Aaron made another choice he hoped would free everyone.

Aaron continued his story, acknowledging he had started the fire to the barns that evening. Telling of how he left Leroy screaming and ranting at nothing and everything, stumbling around the stills. How he retreated back into the woods until he was out of sight upon seeing his father approach to gather more product for the clubs.

Just before dusk, he returned to the production barns with supplies in hand, intending to eliminate the stills for good. Seeing no one was nearby, he struck the match that would end his brother's life. He was not aware Leroy was passed out and unconscious next to the woodpile beside the barn. It was not until he heard his father screaming for Leroy that he knew what he had done. To this day, he regretted not taking that extra moment to have looked around the structures before committing arson. Hearing his father's screams for his brother, Aaron ran across the creek and waited for the right opportunity to reveal himself to Beatrice. Circling around the woods, he settled in to observe the house from the tree break just beyond where Johnny had died. Listening carefully in case his father began to take his anger out on Beatrice. The lamps in the house were dark; Aaron assumed she was safe for one more night.

Returning to the burial grounds, he unearthed the tin box; retrieving the money within, he discarded the box before tidying up the headstones of his family. His car, hidden at the far end of the farm, he returned to it and attempted to rest as best he could through the night.

The next day came and went slowly as he waited for the right time to appear at the shack. Falling back asleep in the warm afternoon sun, he was awakened by the sound of a car approaching. Staying low in the seat where he could not be seen, he saw his father drive past, heading towards the main road. Edgar was off to make his deliveries. With his father now gone, Aaron walked back through the woods to the graves. Approaching the clearing, he spotted his sister sitting between the markers holding his childhood tin box. Seeing her stand up, he waved to her. Gathering up his nerve to approach her, Aaron turned to walk away when he spotted David racing toward her. He decided it was best to let his last wave goodbye to his sister be his last forever.

Aaron was aware Ida had passed and knew of the car David had purchased; these bits of information left him inclined to believe David was making good on the promise made when they last kissed. Knowing he couldn't stay, he decided to go once and for all. This choice allowed everyone to move forward without the risk associated with knowing he was alive.

As the day wore on, the trio from a former life stayed in the small apartment catching up, drinking coffee, and snacking on bagels fresh from the deli. Warm beverages morphed into wine and spirits as the evening drew near. Little Aaron moved in and out of the conversation, switching between toys and adult dialogue. His interest in these new men in his life ebbed and flowed.

Discerning Beatrice was safe and away from Carter County, Aaron chose to leave his country to work the oil fields of Alaska. He used this time to save money, mature in his looks, gain a few scars, and generally become the man he wanted to be. Returning to the States, he decided to call Manhattan home. Considering his past there, this was a bold move, but he considered the island his home. It would be a year before he found his sister living in the same city, separated by only a few blocks; it was not until then he discovered her first baby was gone.

Beatrice asked why he didn't reveal himself sooner. Aaron said he had no excuse; he felt safer being a provider to her without having to explain his life. So many people had rejected him because of whom he chose to love; he wasn't prepared for how she might react. Understanding and acknowledging his concern, she reached across the table to hold his hand.

As all these details meshed together in her head, Beatrice concluded that Aaron would have known Thadeus. She wanted to ask the question but was afraid of the answer.

Was there some remote chance he knew where her adopted family had gone? She still longed to find her firstborn son, to make him aware of who she was and where he had come from.

Aaron continued with various details of his adventures back in the States. The last trip he had taken south was to Texas. He told them of the distributor who ran the bars in the City, a man named Thadeus Johnson. It was indeed a twist of fate that he had run into Thadeus in a hospital in Ranger, Texas.

Aaron received word through a private network that his dear friend, who had saved him, was in the hospital suffering from severe dementia. The judge had left the bitter cold of New York winters, settling in Texas after retiring from the agency.

Aaron surmised his old friend would be languishing alone in the hospital; he needed to wish his friend a fond farewell and decided it would be safe to say his goodbyes to his dear colleague. Leaving the hospital that fateful day, he bumped into a lovely young woman knocking her down. In apologizing to her husband, he recognized the man, who was, in fact, Thadeus.

Beatrice's eyes were wide open with anticipation. Was this the missing piece she needed to find her boy? As

Aaron continued to speak, David put his hand on her arm and took her hand. Both he and Beatrice were intently listening to Aaron speak.

"After I returned from Alaska, I had a few opportunities to connect with old friends I could trust, people outside the government. I was aware of the large bounty on Thadeus from his previous partners. I made the necessary calls, and within a few hours, a trailer full of wood had overturned on Thadeus, killing him instantly. I remained in Texas long enough to attend the funeral and collect the money."

Aaron noticed the sadness overcoming Beatrice. Both she and David stared at him with eyes wide open.

"The Johnson family were the people who took me in when David left me in Oklahoma City. Thadeus and his wife are the people who stole the baby from me when Tom and I moved to Manhattan."

Aaron sat in silence for a few minutes. Thinking through the odd sequence of events.

"It's ironic, isn't it?"

"What is?"

Asked David.

"The bounty for Thadeus paid for her education."

Chapter 18

Beatrice had to decide if she was willing to reopen the search for her son again or not. It had been an emotional drain on her the first time, but how could she not attempt to find her son after receiving the new information from her brother? The thought that she would not locate him was genuine to her; even so, she concluded it was worth the risk.

Turning to David and Aaron, she asked their thoughts. David's detective nature immediately suggested they go to Texas and see what they could uncover. Visit the grave of Thadeus, talk to the caretaker, and ask if he remembered anything. Possibly find a record of where the family resided at the time of his death.

Beatrice deeply felt it was the right thing to do. She and Aaron began immediately packing clothes for their journey. David committed to taking care of the younger Aaron while she and his significant other headed to Texas on the next available plane. Arriving in Dallas, they rented a car to make their way through the Texas hills to the small town of Ranger. Ascending the magnanimous

Ranger Hill, they reached the top and took the first road they came to, which led them to the cemetery. This stop would be futile as Aaron didn't recall what part of the graveyard Thadeus was buried in.

As a means of a kiss goodbye to Thadeus, Aaron was one of the funeral attendees; he vividly recalled how beautiful the grieving widow was and was quite clear there had not been a child attending the services. He mentioned the calm demeanor carried by the widow to Beatrice; she was not surprised to hear there had been no lack of tears for the dead man. Entering the bricked entrance, they immediately drove to the back of the enclosed land, looking for the caretaker's home. Aaron hoped by driving around the cemetery while observing the headstones; his memory would be jogged. His mind, like the caretaker's house, was unyielding of information. Seeing the dilapidated wooden structure, they surmised the home to be vacant. Sitting in the car, staring at the rotting structure, the two grew weary. Exhausted from their journey, they agreed to find a room and rest before continuing their search.

In the small hotel bed, the night was fitful for Beatrice. Her slumber was filled with dreams about the early days of Kenneth in the home where she had been taken in.

She vividly remembered the details of the house; the perfect drapes and its pristine tiled countertops. Between her moments of sleep, she lay awake in her bed, staring at her brother sleeping. Wondering how fate knew she needed him back in her life. Wondering why he finally chose to reveal himself.

Aaron woke and began to dress, not realizing his sister was awake. He was as quiet as possible, for he wanted her to rest. As he was tying his tie, she spoke to him.

"I am so thankful to have you back in my life. This is a dream I would have never imagined would become a reality."

Hearing this made him smile as he was also grateful to interact with his sister beyond being a guardian angel.

Beatrice sat up on the edge of her bed and reached for Aaron's hand. Taking his hand in hers, she inquired why he chose to come back now. Aaron paused before telling her David had been pushing Aaron to let Beatrice know he was alive for some time. Aaron admitted he wasn't willing to take the risk until he had confirmation that Edgar was dead; only then was he willing to reveal himself. Holding each other's gaze, Beatrice concluded how much her brother loved her; she recognized he was willing to forego his own happiness to protect her.

Now that she was awake, he picked up the phone and asked the operator to connect a long-distance call to New York. Hearing his sweetheart answer the phone, he became giddy with love. Confirming all was well with David; he passed the handset to Beatrice so she could speak to her son. Beatrice confirmed Mommy was well and was having a good trip. Knowing her son was having a wonderful time with his new uncle, she relaxed. She smiled at her brother and handed the phone back to him. Aaron wrapped up the call with David confiding how much he missed him, confirming they would be home soon. Hanging up the phone, the reconnected siblings set off in search of breakfast.

Finishing their breakfast, they received the check from the aged waitress; sensing she would be a good source of information, Aaron queried if she knew who was responsible for the cemetery. The server wove a tale of how the county had taken over the land where the caretaker passed away. The city and county coordinated efforts to maintain the property; any resident of the county could purchase a plot for a reasonable fee. She giggled as she spoke of how the local mortuary was furious they could no longer control the cost of the land.

"The greedy bastards went out near the new interstate and purchased several acres for burials. If you want them to bury you, you would have to buy a plot on their land! Any-who, anything you want to know about the original cemetery, you can find out from the county clerk."

Paying their bill and leaving a generous tip for the help they received, they proceeded to the county courthouse, where the clerk confirmed the cemetery information was archived in the courthouse basement. The young clerk corroborated the waitress' story, reiterating that after the caretaker passed away, the city and county took over the graveyard. Escorting the pair down the marble stairs towards the basement, the clerk explained what information they could retrieve on their own and what information would have to be searched for by request. During their research, they discovered the plot number and area of the cemetery Thadeus was buried in. Finding that information, they replaced the books on the shelves and proceeded up the stairs to the main floor. Before leaving, they asked the helpful clerk working for the county how they might obtain the address of the widow Johnson. The county clerk handed them the form required while making a note of the necessary fee. Aaron paid the bill while Beatrice filled out the document to the best of her knowledge.

Submitting their request, they exited the courthouse and drove directly to the cemetery. Parking just inside the main gate, the pair walked hand in hand up the center drive to find the grave where Thadeus now resided. Approaching the headstone, they noted it was a double headstone with a place for Mary to be placed at the time of her passing. Her name and birthdate were already carved into the granite; all that was missing was the death date. Looking at every detail of the headstone, it struck Beatrice what a lavish stone it was. Mary must have spent a significant amount of money on the marker; she temporarily utilized her degree to analyze the importance. Was it vanity, or was there more to the couple who befriended her? Looking back, she wondered what other secrets their household must have kept.

Standing next to his sister in deep thought, Aaron was the first one to see the placard with Baby Johnson written on it. Observing the sign, he gently took his sister's hand into his while pointing out the sign to her. Feeling her hand tighten in his, he pulled her close and held her while she cried for her lost child.

Returning to the car, he asked if she wanted to find the woman who had taken him.

Beatrice paused before responding.

"I feel Mary has probably suffered enough. No conversation between us could possibly heal the wounds we have endured."

Somewhat deflated, she reached for his hand and patted it.

"Let's just go home."

Chapter 19

Mary moved in and out of consciousness for several weeks, mumbling out loud, conversations held within her deep sleep. To bystanders, it appeared she was being visited by those who had gone before her, spirits from the afterlife she had encountered while they were alive. Sometimes the words passing her lips were argumentative; often, they were shy and frightened. Once in a while, the words spoken were accompanied by a smile. Little bits here and there were intelligible but nothing listeners deemed relevant, mostly due to the fact her life prior to Ranger was unknown to anyone here, including her son. Mary made a conscious choice to never talk about life before Ranger, Texas. John Edward knew little of his mother's past, and his memories of his dad were slight. The electric shock which had traveled through his body as a young boy erased many of his early memories. On occasion, vague recollections from when he was very young appeared in dreams. When he shared these with his mother, she was quick to dismiss the images in his head. Making it very clear to him that there was nothing of importance that needed recalling.

Bettie entered the room at nine that morning, committed to staying with Mary while John Edward went home to rest. Even with all the history between them, John Edward knew he could trust his ex-wife with his mother's well-being. When she arrived in the room, putting her purse and craftwork down next to the chair, she and her ex-husband shared a cordial moment, conversing over Mary's current state of being. John Edward shared the latest news from the doctor, which was nothing new.

"She talks in her sleep about nonsense, gibberish making no sense to me. I suspect she is working out something she needs to finalize before she goes."

Shaking his head in sadness, tossing his inherited sandy blonde hair softly in tandem with his head, John Edward said goodbye to his ex-wife as he left the room. Stopping at the door before he exited, he turned to face Bettie.

"The box on the window sill is for you from Mother. I found a note on her nightstand at home. Hand-written instructions to pass these to you upon her death. I believe her days are few, so I retrieved them yesterday. I think you'll look lovely wearing them."

It was around eleven-thirty when an aide delivered a tray of food for Mary, a pointless act as she never consumed any of the liquids presented to her. Bettie chatted with the young woman carrying the liquids, mostly about the weather. In particular, how quickly fall seemed to be approaching. She continued to speak of how summer had been unseasonably cool for Texas, causing many to agree that winter would likely be harsh with unusually cold temperatures. The aide finished arranging the tray; removing the straw from its white paper wrapper, she placed it in the glass of watered-down iced tea. Bettie watched and wondered why this ritual was continually repeated; it was the perfect example of insanity.

Bettie continued organizing her yarn to start on her crochet when she was startled.

"Is she gone?"

Mary managed to grumble the small sentence out of her parched mouth. Bettie wasn't sure if she was awake or calling out in one of her dreams.

"Could you raise the damn bed? I am tired of laying flat!"

Mary commanded in complete coherence, direct and forward as always. Bettie was now fully aware her mother-in-law was, indeed, awake.

She had heard stories of people coming back from an incoherent state after their bodies thoroughly rested; she wasn't quite sure what to think. She rose from the chair near the window. Shuffling across the tile floor in her bare feet, she raced to the bed controls hanging from the polished metal bed rails. Observing the buttons, she pushed the one that would raise the head of the bed. As the bed finally began to rise, Mary shifted her frail body slightly. Being severely atrophied, she exerted a large amount of effort for this minor repositioning. Mary's muscles had become so weak it was near impossible for her to move without assistance. In an almost upright position, Mary looked at the tray with its avocado-colored melamine dishes, each filled with pureed food-like liquids.

"Are they still bringing me this shit? This is supposed to heal the sick. Yuck!"

With what strength she had left, she pushed the tray away in disgust. Bettie recognized the familiar behavior of the woman lying in that bed. Her former mother-in-law seemingly returned from the dead, the woman with whom she had battled for so many years.

"Let me call John Edward; he will want to be here."

As Bettie reached for the phone, Mary shook her head side to side to indicate no. She looked at Bettie before taking a deep breath and beginning to speak.

"There are things I need to tell you. It is necessary I make sure this is heard before I go. I don't want John Edward to know this while I am still alive. I trust you will carry this burden for me until the time is right to tell him."

Mary's voice was clear; her speech concise. She raised a feeble hand reaching for the glass of tea on her tray. Placing the phone's handset back on its base, Bettie moved the beverage towards the edge of the tray table; Mary leaned her frail body forward and took a sip.

Having earlier heard Mary speak of the Smith family, of whom she had been utterly unaware of any relations, Bettie was now intrigued as to what it was Mary needed to tell her. What was so important to share that it was keeping her alive? She couldn't imagine anything Mary could say to her that would cause that great of a shock to anyone. Obviously important enough for Mary to keep fighting death, Bettie prepared herself for the information. Grabbing her pen and pad from her purse, she prepared to jot down notes.

Mary picked right up where she had left off earlier, telling Bettie about the family and the grand life they lived. She spoke of her mother and the cruelties thrust upon her by her stepfather. She recanted about the events leading up to meeting her savior, Mrs. Simpson. Mary spoke fondly of the nurse who risked her lively hood to save a scared young girl. Moved by the story she was sharing, she shed a single tear; the small amount of saline moving down her cheek was all her arid body could manage to produce. Bettie sensed the sadness welling up in Mary as she proceeded to disclose the past.

"I betrayed someone in the cruelest way possible; I built up their trust and then took the one thing that truly belonged to them."

As Mary disclosed the plan she and Thadeus had put into place, Bettie sat in shock, no longer carving the words into the notepad.

Mary continued describing how they moved from town to town, how Thadeus bribed the state judge to alter the birth records, and every detail of the life they built right up to the time of John Edward's father's mysterious death.

The afternoon passed quickly as Mary provided copious amounts of information to her former daughter-in-law. Mary stopped speaking when she noticed Bettie looking at her watch. Amazed at the amount of time that had passed, Bettie stood to stretch her legs. Turning back to the bed, she found Mary beginning to fade back into her slumber. Bettie reached for the bed controls to return the mattress to its horizontal position. Mary looked at her.

"Where's John Edward? I want to see him before I go back to sleep."

As Bettie reached for the phone to find John Edward, he entered the room as if on cue. He was elated to see his mother awake. His eyes filled with tears seeing her coherent. He quickly crossed the room to her bedside and leaned down, resting his head on her barren chest. Bettie picked up her crochet, notepad, and pen and prepared to leave. She wanted to give them as much time as possible together; she also needed time to soak up the information shared with her that afternoon.

Picking up the blue-colored box of jewelry among her belongings, she moved towards the hallway door to exit the room. Just as she passed the door frame, she heard Mary.

"Do the right thing!"

A smile came to her lips while she quietly stated out loud,

"That's the woman I remember."

Stopping in the hallway to collect herself, she heard mother and son engage in conversation. Only now did Bettie understand why Mary had always interacted with people as she did. Mary had committed her life to control what she could to protect her son. The warmth in her had been locked away, hidden, out of necessity.

Chapter 20

The completion of her doctorate opened doors and windows beyond Beatrice's wildest dreams. In the following years, she continually worked, letting passion be her guide. The more she helped others, the more full her life was. Having the two lovely Aarons and David with her fulfilled her heart to the point where she consciously chose to never marry again. Her work, along with her family, satisfied her emotional needs.

Anyone seeking her help became one of her children. Beatrice became a mom to many through the years. In her mid-forties, she began collating information about all her children, a chronicle of people lost in the world seeking personal salvation. Just as David told her of his plight when he was a young boy, she used the written collection to show other victims; they were not alone. Beatrice took great pride in what she had accomplished; this feeling of reward pushed her to continually expand her education and spend most waking moments in discovery mode.

Many people adored her, both those who knew her personally and others who were merely observers. The work she was involved in fed her soul, sustaining contentment in the life she lived. Among the many opportunities presented to her, the most coveted one was the chance to write a column for The Times. It would become one of the most respected and well-read columns ever syndicated. Her written opinion, revered by those who believed in her, shaped her as a Truth Speaker. Her mantra, developed from many years of service, was; you must walk through life's pain, acknowledge and own it if you are to find a path beyond it.

Beatrice was honored on her sixty-third birthday with a Black Tie Gala. Story after story was shared by the people she helped through the years. She considered everyone in that room a friend; the love emanating through the air was beyond her wildest dreams. The elder Aaron, now in his seventies, took the podium to speak of his beloved David and how his sister had openly honored their love, a symbol of her true spirit and compassion for all mankind.

"It was through her vision and tenacity each of us is here this evening; my devoted sister endured more pain and sorrow than any of you know. She chose not to share her past; the evil that pursued her in her early years remained a secret so she could focus on helping others. David once gave her words of wisdom, which provided her hope and a vision. I will be forever thankful to him for planting this seed in her and forever grateful to Beatrice for how she grew from that bit of wisdom."

Aaron continued sharing his admiration for his sister and the bond they shared. Everyone in attendance that night bore witness to the love they had for one another.

"In Lower Manhattan, an apartment building containing sixteen single-unit apartments was recently purchased with the intent to serve abuse victims. Anyone needing a place to heal emotionally, regardless of race, sexual orientation, or ability to pay, will be served. Families in need of a place to live so they might exit the violent situation they are in, and any person suffering from violence will be served. Counselors will be available twenty-four-seven, servicing needs at any time. It was my beloved David's dying wish that his estate was utilized to support this endeavor. Thanks to his contribution, the building is now wholly owned and free of any financial obligations. As a tribute to my sister and the amazing work she has done, the building will bear her name. In Beatrice's honor, all the proceeds raised tonight will provide financial support for servicing those in need. In addition, a non-profit group was recently established, and the board of directors has been charged with overseeing the day-to-day operations along with aligning strategic expansion plans for the growth of this amazing facility."

Aaron paused while the crowd jubilantly applauded. He looked at his sister with a beaming smile of pride on his face.

He continued sharing stories about his sister, some funny, some surreal.

"With all this said, please continue your applause for the woman who made this a reality, Board President Beatrice Torrez."

Humbled by the gift of admiration, Beatrice rose from her seat at a table near the podium. She became keenly aware the audience grew silent in anticipation of what she would share on this momentous occasion. Beatrice floated across the stage in her simple black velour evening gown with gold satin piping as if being carried by angels. To a certain extent, she was. The affection of all the angels in the room carried her, both those alive as well as the spirits from the past. Arriving at the microphone, Beatrice stopped to absorb the moment before speaking. She arranged the mic while staring out, attempting to see her dear friends shadowed by the spotlight. The room grew silent, waiting for her, only for her.

"It is because of each of you and your tireless work and kind donations that we are here tonight to celebrate. This celebration is not about me turning another year older; it is about how I have been allowed one more year to help someone else find the joy they have been missing. As I prepared for this evening, I looked back to my youth growing up in Oklahoma to the long journey delivering me to this spot, to this moment in time. I think of the people I have laughed with and, more importantly, the people I have cried with. I am reminded of something I was told so very long ago. My brother-in-law David shared his truth with me, which gave me insight. A knowledge that sparked a fire in me, pushing me to always grow and learn about what I don't understand."

She took a long moment to pause before requesting the spotlight be turned off, so she could see past the podium. She once again assessed the crowd of rich and poor, African-Americans, Caucasians, Latinos, heads of state, housewives, gay, straight, married, single, multiple generations, all of whom were in attendance. Silence was her friend as she chose her next words with care.

"This group is a perfect example of life's polarity allowing us to function; to maintain balance, opposites must exist. If not for the bad we encounter, we would not recognize the good. I have been the recipient of many saviors in my life, as I believe we all have. But the one I would like to remember at this moment of gratitude is a dear woman who altered my life in a way I would have never expected. I will not bore you with this story of why or the circumstances around the act but will only say to her, 'Thank you for what you took from me,' it was with this loss that I was compelled to reach out and help those in need."

"My dear sweet Mary, wherever you are, I thank you, and please know you are forgiven."

Floating above the crowd, unseen by all the party guests, Mary smiled, knowing she had been forgiven. To her right, she caught a glimpse of a handsome man flashing his capturing smile at her. Thadeus had come to collect her and guide her to their next adventure.

Beatrice sensed Mary's presence nearby. Feeling her spirit in the room, Bea blew a kiss upward through the air. Although she could not see Mary, she sensed the kiss had landed on her cheek as intended.

As she ascended into the heavens, Mary's soul was finally at peace.

Chapter 21

Mom and I remained seated across from each other in the bistro, me listening intently to her, unable to speak. The information she shared was overwhelming, something out of a movie. As fate would have it, I was the grandchild of two amazing women who did what they had to do to survive. Gaining perspective as to why my grandmother behaved as she did was shocking. Hearing of the childhood atrocities she faced, it all made sense now. Shifting in my chair in the noisy restaurant, I looked around at everyone living their lives, pondering who needed to be helped and who required healing. Had we all just become cogs in the wheels of the daily grind? How many of us really spent time walking through our pain to find healing? Who of us is under a loved one's control and doesn't know how to get out?

Glancing at my watch, I was surprised to see three hours had passed; I had listened the entire time while my mom told the stories of these two amazing women.

That day's new information shared lit a small flame in me that would grow, eventually changing my life forever. As my mom looked at me, she smiled with a look only a mother can give, a smile of love and hope.

Settling our bill with an extra-large gratuity to the waiter for his time, I pushed back from the table, stretched, and escorted my mom to her car. I needed to thank my mother for sharing this story with me and also thank her for being kind enough to develop respect for my grandmother after so many years.

Taking the car keys out of my mother's hand, I unlocked her door. Before handing the keys back to her, I opened her door and waited for her to take the driver's seat. She stood beside the car for a moment, looking for the words she needed to say before settling in. Looking at me and smiling, she explained how Grandmother's jewelry came into her care.

"Mary had left a note for your dad to retrieve them from her safety deposit box. She had two purposes in giving them to me. One was to present them as a gift to say thanks, acknowledging the hard feelings between us through the years, and two, requesting they be passed on to her grandchildren. In addition to the jewelry, an envelope addressed to you was given to me."

Continuing with how Grandmother acknowledged the desire to reach out to Beatrice but never managed enough courage to do it.

"Your grandmother followed Bea's career until her final visit to the hospital last year. Often after reading her column in the paper, your grandmother would make an anonymous cash donation to any foundation mentioned in Beatrice's article. Mary could never be sure how your dad would receive the information and couldn't bear the thought of losing him after all these years. She assured me all the money left from your grandfather was spent supporting Bea's causes. Now I understand her pain and how difficult the decision was for her to share this story with me before she passed."

Softly touching my hand from beside the car, she said,

"Son, promise me you will never hide your light. Never carry shame for what others have done to you."

After she was settled in the driver's seat, I closed her car door and began to walk away. She gently tapped her horn to get my attention, and when I turned, she had rolled down her window.

"In her final hours, your grandmother had become surprisingly lucid, fully aware of her surroundings. It was obvious to me that the time for her to go was near. I said my farewells and moved away from the bed to leave that room for the last time. Standing in the hallway, I heard her speak to your father, 'You were my greatest gift in life. If my journey had to be hard - I am forever grateful I had the love of my life with me through it all. I could not have imagined a greater dance partner.' I returned home that afternoon, reflecting on life. Sitting at the kitchen table, admiring the jewelry she left for me, the phone rang. It was your dad on the other end of the line informing me Mary was gone. He said her final words were odd to him but thought I would understand what they meant."

Through his tears, my father repeated his mother's last words on this earth.

"Mom held my hand firmly, and closing her eyes; she said, 'Forgive me, Beatrice, forgive me...'"

The End

This is the first novel written by Danielle Parks.

This work has been produced in Audiobook and Podcast formats; both are available at P1Press.co.

Other titles available through P1Press are:

The Girl Who Stole My Chair!

My Life Being A Sensitive

8 Things You Should Know To Launch A Product Line

Ready To Own A Salon? 10 Things You Should Know

P1Press

ISBN 978-1-7329729-7-1

www.ingramcontent.com/pod-product-compliance
Lightning Source LLC
Chambersburg PA
CBHW021105110726
47900CB00007B/2037